D1626805

## LEFT OF CENTRE

What happens when a young Englishman, of conventional upbringing and 'sensible' liberal views, goes to Paris to complete his education. Normally, precious little.

But for Henry Arnold (late of Cranpole, Trinity and the Third Flintshires) it was different. For one thing, the time was Spring 1958, with France on the verge of revolution. For another, though Henry was fairly unassuming, he had a habit of getting involved with people. With, for instance, Dora, the pneumatic mixed-up spouse of the Rock 'n' Roll Peer. With Madame la Fouette's right-wing political salon and with Sir Rupert Fitzhoward, the Anglo-Irish propagandist of the Quai d'Orsay. Above all, with Cleo, the ravishing young heiress who set out to beat the Fascists single-handed.

In his first, fizzling—but not entirely frivolous— novel, Paul Johnson presents Paris in the twilight of the Fourth Republic. Henry meets the characters who make it the most exciting capital in the world: the storm-police and society spivs, the poets and politicians, the painters and pornographers, the journalists and fashion-models. He finds himself completing his education in Left Bank flats and Right Bank palaces, in the editorial offices of *France-Miracle*—even in the headquarters of the Communist Party. *Left of Centre*, in short, describes the meeting of a Complacent Young Man with an Angry Old City.

# Paul Johnson

# LEFT OF CENTRE

LONDON
MACGIBBON & KEE
1959

TO JACKIE

# FOREWORD

This novel is a work of pure fiction. Though it takes place against the background of a series of political events which did, in fact, occur, none of the characters is based, either in whole or in part, on real persons, living or dead. The names of certain politicians are mentioned merely to add colour and authenticity; I do not wish to imply that they were really involved with any of my characters.

PAUL JOHNSON

# I

'PASSENGERS travelling to Paris by BEA Viscount Flight Number 488 kindly board the aircraft for immediate departure. Have your boarding cards ready. No smoking until we are airborne, please'. Henry Arnold rose from his Martian foam-rubber armchair and joined the shuffling group of passengers as they squeezed through the door of the departure lounge.

He was heavily burdened. Despite the early Spring sunshine, he was wearing his buff-coloured British Warm, to save weight in his luggage allowance, a bowler hat, cocked at a rakish angle over his thick blond hair, and a Trinity College scarf. Under one arm was a tightly rolled umbrella, Volume One of *A la Recherche du Temps Perdu* (in French, and with only the first four pages cut), Professor Brogan's *The Development of Modern France*, and a pair of bedroom slippers, which somehow had got left out of his bags. Under the other arm was Michel Butor's new novel (completely uncut) and copies of *France-Observateur*, *Esprit*, *Les Temps Modernes* and last Sunday's *Observer* which, though it was now Wednesday, he had not yet entirely succeeded in digesting. Somewhere in his bulging pockets, stuffed with gloves, letters, aspirins, Alka-Seltzer and a bottle of cough-mixture, were a passport, boarding card and £100 in traveller's cheques. Henry, in short, was off to take a six months' *Cours de Civilisation* at the Sorbonne, preparatory to starting on life's great adventure.

His tall, slim, slightly stooping figure, crowned by a

7

long, pale face from which a bony nose protruded with earnest enquiry, gave him a sufficiently intellectual air. But National Service in a safe and responsible County regiment had clothed him, outwardly at least, with a conventional skin, and not even three years at Oxford, during which he had gradually discarded his Army friends, had sufficed to rid him of his military chrysalis. He now felt he stood at some great crossroads, one road leading to a Lloyd's brokerage and a family house in Esher, the other to . . . but he was not quite sure. The reputation of a witty and successful playwright, perhaps, with a penthouse in Arlington House and a warren of starlet girl-friends. Or an established novelist's flat in Albany, with the hint of a villa in Cap Ferrat to come. Or even just rooms in Bloomsbury, while he selflessly and laboriously carved out the principles of a new art-form. In his imagination, he saw the diverging roads as the paths which led across the Common from his parents' house in Wimbledon. As a child, going to nursery school, he had always taken the right hand path, safe, comfortable and unexciting; but there had also been a path to the left, which remained unexplored if not forbidden. Somehow, throughout his twenty-four years, he had never had a chance to take the left-hand path. Was he about to take it now? He was not sure. But he was convinced that his six months in Paris would enable him to make up his mind. Paris would provide the signpost.

His father, a burly, successful barrister, with a loud taste in port (which Henry detested), a first-rate golf handicap (ditto) and pronounced Tory opinions (Henry was a liberal who regarded the Suez business as a moral outrage), had been strongly opposed to 'this Paris nonsense' as he called it. He had not wished to force

8

Henry into business—he had long ago abandoned his project of installing him in Chambers—but he had repeatedly stated that his son ought to buckle down immediately to something. He had, however, been firmly overruled by Henry's mother, a woman of frail beauty and considerable sensitivity, who, as the daughter of a famous and worldly portrait painter, was allowed to hold strong opinions on Art, Life and Ambition. From the start she had approved of Henry's wish to spend six months in Paris, and, since Arnold Senior could not reasonably raise any financial objection—he had a first rate practice and anyway, as he had loudly boasted, had just made a killing in television shares—his project had gone through without much fuss. It was generally agreed, however, that Henry should return with firm and detailed views on a career.

Henry had thus been given £100, with the promise of a further £100 at the end of three months. A room had also been booked for him at a small Left-bank hotel, where his mother had stayed thirty years ago, and which she said was much patronized by artists, writers and men of future consequence. Henry was not familiar with the city, though he had passed through it several times on undergraduate expeditions to Italy; but he had read Hemingway, Elliot Paul and *Les Mandarins*; he knew that it was better to eat in a *bistro* than a *restaurant*; that a *brasserie* was not a place which sold women's underclothes; that *Le Canard Enchaîné*, though incomprehensible, was the funniest paper in Europe; that Scandinavian girls in Paris were mostly nymphomaniacs and French girls unattainable; and, finally, that nobody who actually lived in Paris ever went to the Louvre. He was very much looking forward to the whole thing.

In the aircraft, Henry obtained a window-seat from which the view was not totally hidden by the wing, and put on his safety belt. The engines revved; then there was some sort of commotion at the entrance to the plane, and the Air Hostess walked up the passageway, escorting a young woman whom she placed in the seat next to Henry. Out of the corner of his eye, Henry caught a glimpse of long, slender legs, superbly shod in black, high-heeled shoes with diamanté buckles, and terminating in a black silk skirt from which protruded a whisper of frilly petticoats. He heard the flick of a lighter, and turned to see the girl nonchalantly lighting a cigarette. She had sombre red hair, heavily pencilled eyebrows and smouldering grey eyes. She was both raffish and pretty.

'You're not supposed to smoke until the aircraft takes off', said Henry.

'Bloody damn', said the girl crossly, stretching out a thin, scarlet-nailed hand to stub out her cigarette. 'I seem to do everything wrong, don't I? First I nearly miss the plane, then I lose my ticket, and then the customs people mistake me for a drug smuggler or something. Such a sordid, beady-eyed woman asked me questions.'

'Really?' said Henry. 'How exciting.'

The girl turned to look Henry full in the face. 'Do you normally make remarks in that prissy tone of voice?' she asked crossly. Her speech was crisp and educated, but there was a hint of cockney twang underneath. Her glance rested on Henry's British Warm. 'And why are you wearing that ridiculous coat-thing? Have you just come out of the Army?'

'Now look here—' said Henry nervously. After the event, he always felt he ought to get the better of odd encounters like this with young women; he had, he knew, a sharp line in verbal repartee, at any rate with his brother officers and the men in his college. But women both fascinated and terrified him, and he usually found it took a good deal of time, and several drinks if possible, before he could talk to them freely. 'As a matter of fact', he said lamely, 'it's three years since I was in the army. And anyway', he added, plucking up courage, 'why are you wearing a cocktail dress at 11.30 in the morning?'

The girl's good temper returned, and she slid Henry a coy smile. 'Because I didn't go to bed last night, silly. And that, if you want to know, is why I'm looking like a rag doll that's just been in the washing machine, so no dirty cracks, please.'

Definitely a little vulgar, thought Henry. But interesting. He felt his new, Paris-bound confidence expanding. The plane taxied down the runway, and lurched off into the clear March sky.

'Ooh!' said the girl. 'Awful.' She lit another cigarette, and puffed smoke at Henry. 'We're up in the air, so I can smoke now, can't I? What's your name, pretty boy?'

Henry had never been called pretty boy before. 'Henry Arnold,' he said blushingly.

'Mine's Lady Treffle,' said the girl. 'That surprises you, doesn't it? My husband's the Rock-'n'-Roll Peer. Or rather ex-husband.' She laughed. 'Or rather I don't know whether he really *is* my ex-husband, we're in such a legal tangle. Apparently we haven't been married long enough to get divorced—sounds odd, doesn't it? We're legally separated or something like that. But the judge said he had to give me lots of money so *that's* all right.'

Henry was distinctly shocked, despite his cherished liberal views, by what he regarded as a frivolous attitude to an important social problem, but he was not prepared to show it. 'I'm in favour of divorce law reform,' he said, in his serious voice.

'Super,' said the girl. 'And now let's have a drink. Mine's a large Scotch on the Rocks.'

The stewardess brought them two large whiskies. The girl told Henry that her Christian name was Dora, that she was an actress of sorts, that she had a flat in the Rue Jacob and an English boy-friend who was currently in St. Tropez. She had flown over to London for a party, but was now going to settle down seriously to learn French. Henry said that he was going over to Paris to learn French too, and French civilization, of course. She said how nice, perhaps they might have lessons together. He said what a good idea. They had two more whiskies, and by the time the Viscount touched down at Le Bourget, Henry had arranged to come to her flat for drinks before dinner.

They parted at Les Invalides, after a good deal of fuss and bother over Dora's luggage. Henry saw her to a taxi and she blew him a kiss as it drove off. He decided to go to his hotel by Metro—the drinks on the plane had proved quite expensive, and he'd told himself that his life in Paris, at least to begin with, was to be spartan and disciplined. A sandwich for lunch, no drinks before the evening—at any rate after today—at least six hours of reading or lectures every day except Sunday, a classical play once a week, a daily exhibition or museum. As for Dora—but here was a problem. Henry decided he did not like Dora very much, but that he found her very attractive. She was an entirely new phenomenon to him. His previous experience of women had been confined to a jolly colonel's daughter in Malta, with whom he had

12

played tennis, and whom he had kissed after a regimental dance; a rather serious philosophy student from Somerville, who had permitted him certain liberties but who had made it plain that she preferred conversation to sex; and a blonde art student in North Oxford, with whom he had had a brief, uncomfortable and altogether unsatisfactory affair. Each of these three women had, in one way or another, involved him in a lot of trouble, and Henry had come to the reluctant conclusion that, for him at any rate, women always led to disaster. But this did not prevent him from pursuing them, even though he knew the results were likely to be meagre and disappointing. With the casual intrusion of Dora into his life, however, he felt he was entering into a new phase. Unlike the three women he had known previously, she was distinctly glamorous; the sort of female who clearly existed in small quantities, who were usually seen around with people like the Marquis of Milford Haven and Aly Khan, and whose faces were normally glimpsed only in illustrations to William Hickey or Paul Tanfield (Henry did not read *The Tatler*, on principle). She was exciting, reckless, and plainly accessible (Henry did not put much store by the boy-friend in St. Tropez, who seemed a nebulous figure). Yet if he sought to develop their relationship, would she not prove a major obstacle to his pursuit of the *Cours de Civilisation*? And if dull girls brought him trouble, how much more would she bring him? She would, undoubtedly, prove expensive.

He was still pursuing these thoughts when he reached his hotel, which was called the Paris-Palace, in the Rue de Loup off the Boulevard St. Germain. The proprietress, who introduced herself as Madame Marcourt, greeted him warmly and got straight down to business.

13

'You have been given, *jeune homme*, a fine room, full of air and spaciousness', she said, speaking rapid French in a strong Toulousaine accent. 'It has a new mattress, and the linoleum is only one year old. Your next-door neighbour is a Communist *député*, who is a man of quiet and regular habits, *très sérieux*, and will not disturb you. Reciprocally, you will appreciate that he is a man of great responsibilities who has many papers to read at night, so you are asked to observe due silence. Your room costs 500 francs a day, *taxes et service comprises*, and is payable weekly. After three months, you are entitled to a statutory reduction of 20 per cent, and the room is then payable monthly. You will not hang up pictures except with the drawing pins. And you must not *faire la cuisine* in your room, or introduce electrical apparatus. If you wish to bring home a girl there is an additional charge of 100 francs a night. The chambermaid is called Odette, and her *pudeur* is to be respected. The hotel does not serve *petit déjeuner*, but there is an excellent café next door run by my brother-in-law, a man who has been trained in the best Swiss hotels.'

This, thought Henry, was really getting down to life in Paris. He whistled cheerfully as he arranged his things (the air and spaciousness in his room were very relative, and the new mattress iron-hard, but this was as it should be and he rejoiced in his coming attic existence). Afterwards, he walked slowly through the sun-dappled streets to the Café Mabillon and ordered a Gruyère sandwich and a large café-crème. The trees were opening out, people were beginning to sit at the pavement tables, Spring was in the air; politics were approaching the crisis-season—the headline in *France-Soir* read: *Le Ministère Gaillard Menacé*. Henry knew little about French politics, and what little he knew he disapproved of. Their constitution was clearly unworkable, and most French deputies appeared to lack a sense of national responsibility. Their policy in Algeria, as the *Observer* had pointed out time and time again, was not only morally reprehensible but totally unrealistic. Henry suspected that Proportional Representation—which theoretically he considered perhaps the most equitable voting system—was probably at the root of France's difficulties. But, as Professor Brogan had observed, the *scrutin uninominal à deux tours*, which had been in force under the Third Republic, was not very successful either.

Henry was not primarily interested in politics, but he had definite and carefully considered views. A supporter of the Welfare State, he believed that nationalisation was now irrelevant, that the Greek case in Cyprus was basically sound, that we should 'come to terms with the Arabs', examine with care the Rapacki proposals, implement the Wolfenden report (though he recognized that its recommendations on prostitution were more a palliative than a cure), abolish capital punishment and restrict commercial advertising on television. He could not make up his mind about the H-bomb, but was quite sure that Nato was a regrettable necesssity.He approved of the Council of Europe, Unesco and the Eleven Plus. In his first year at Oxford, the excesses of Bevanism had led him to join the Liberal Party, but now he was a firm supporter of Mr. Gaitskell and had read with care and approval Mr. Anthony Crosland's important book, *The Future of Socialism*. His heroes were Lord Altrincham, Victor Gollancz and Mr. Douglas Jay. Though not a member of any church, he had read Professor C. S. Lewis' theological works, and was by no means a con-

vinced agnostic. He was inclined to believe in some form
of guiding providence, but quite prepared to wait for
age and experience to shape his views. In fact, as he
sometimes remarked jokingly, he was the *homme moyen
libéral*, though privately he considered he had a logical
and inquiring mind, which led him to sound and
reasonable conclusions on most aspects of human
existence.

Dora Treffle's flat in the Rue Jacob was on the third
floor of a decaying seventeenth century house overlooking a large garden. At six-thirty, Henry, still wearing his
blue London suit, strode up the echoing wooden stairs
and rapped on her door. He had still not decided what
tactics he would adopt towards her, and was inclined,
for the moment, to let events take their natural course.

The door was opened by a small, duffle-coated man,
with sharp protruding teeth and long black hair. He
gave Henry a glance in which suspicion was mingled
with apprehension.

'Isn't this Lady Treffle's flat?' asked Henry.

'An Englishman, thank God', said the small man.
'Wearing that suit I thought you were a gent from the
*Préfecture*. Come on in. Dora's just mixing the drinks.'

He led Henry through a small, cluttered hall into a
vast studio sitting-room in a state of primeval chaos.
An oaken refectory table was covered with bottles and
books. There were violent *tâchiste* paintings, mostly
unframed, on the walls and a massive and unspeakable
piece of sculpture in one corner. Dresses and underclothes hung wildly over the armchairs. Great stacks of
books overflowed from the bookshelves and lay in piles
on the floor. There was an unmade bed, on which a

bearded man was sitting, eating sardines out of a tin. Dora, who had changed into tight black satin trousers and a boyish white shirt, squatted on the floor mixing a cocktail in a large earthenware bowl.

'Welcome to squalor,' she called to Henry. 'And meet Artie, the bearded person here, who is supposed to be painting my portrait and is unfortunately American. And this', she said, pointing to the small, sharp man, 'is Edgar Offrey, true-blue Englishman, Communist and poet. They have been wrecking my flat during the week-end, but in about an hour's time I'm going to throw them out and we'll have dinner. Meanwhile, I'm preparing a delicious drink of my own invention which I've christened Madame Krushchev's Breath, because it's got vodka in it. Also calvados, white wine, grape-juice and just a spot of crème de menthe. No bloody ice unfortunately. Want some?'

'Please,' said Henry, though he disliked cocktails. He removed a brassière from a red plush armchair and sat down. The cocktail tasted very strong and unpleasant and he was aware that Edgar the poet was subjecting him to a hostile stare.

'What, pray, are you supposed to be doing in this city?' he finally asked Henry. He had a voice like coal being crunched underfoot.

'Henry's going to study French civilization,' volunteered Dora.

'Ha!' said Edgar, seizing his cue. 'Another immaculate product of our public schools come to rub his nose in the welcoming dirt. Invisible decay searching out visible decay. The English bourgeoisie always choose Paris as the place to lose their social virginity, because they can pretend they are doing it in the name of culture. Admit

17

it, man! You came to Paris to drink and whore, so that eventually when you return to England and acquire a stockbroker's villa and a partnership in Lloyd's, you will have something to make lewd hints about to your odious and adoring future wife.'

'Why did you think I was a policeman?' asked Henry.

'Because, dear idiot, I am accustomed to smoke marijuana cigarettes—ah! I see that shocks you—and the police take an interest in these things. But to return to civilization. You will find none of it here. The trappings, yes. The middlemen of civilization—the Buffets, the Sagans, the Sartres—yes, again, in their thousands. The philistines who get vicarious satisfaction from associating with the civilized, like Dora here, these also you will find. Even the would-be civilized savages, like our wretched Artie, and other refugees from Dulles—they are here in abundance too. But French civilization itself? It died with Valéry. It has yet to be reborn. France is like the body of a woman with undelivered children in her belly. The only way you can release them is by desecrating the corpse and tearing them out. We must hope that the day is coming when this will be done.'

'How much of your poetry has been published?' asked Henry, a little cruelly as he thought.

'You thought to embarrass me by that question', replied Edgar. 'You were mistaken. The answer is: a great deal, mainly in obscure journals of which you have never heard. But I have not projected myself upon the public because I have yet to decide the role I am to assume. Since we live in an era of moral oblivion, I have no scruple in performing a confidence trick on society, partly to revenge myself on it, partly to enable it to give me a living—and a good one, too. But it takes time and serious thought to decide what trick to play. The boozing-Celtic-Dylan Thomas trick? The ex-Communist - Congress - of - Cultural - Freedom - Stephen Spender trick? The angry-John Osborne trick? The despair-nonsense-Sam Beckett trick? Or even a new trick? It will be at least another year before my mind is made up. Then I shall strike, and strike hard. I shall acquire money, fame and influence, and a position in society from which I will be able to wreak the maximum damage on it.'

'Meanwhile', drawled Artie, 'he lives off kind-hearted females like her ladyship here. They find him soothing because he talks on and on in a vaguely cultural way which they can't understand but makes them feel good, and at the same time he doesn't take up any of their sexual attention.'

'A characteristically crude Texan remark', said Edgar, 'and, equally characteristically, erroneous. I accept Dora's hospitality, when offered, but I am quite capable of earning—as indeed I *do* earn—my own living. Once or twice a year, I am paid 300,000 francs by a French publisher for writing a volume of pornographic literature of the type sold in large quantities to American and British tourists and doubtless also to persons such as this young gentleman here. Such work is easy, yet, being purely imaginative in nature, excellent training for a poet. From time to time I insert passages of political and literary criticism and even poetry in these novels. The publisher doesn't like it, but I am quite adamant that he should not cut a line, and I point out to him that such passages are the nearest approach to literature that his clients are ever likely to read: this appeals to his French bourgeois sense of cultural obligation. I therefore regard these books of mine with some pride.'

'*Strange Tastes*,' said Dora, '*The Endless Night* and *The Permanent Erection*. I've read them all. Lousy, the lot of them.'

'I would remind you', said Edgar crossly, 'that *Strange Tastes* went into six editions and sold at least 100,000 copies. It's been publicly burned in twenty-nine countries, denounced by Birmingham magistrates and discovered in a duchess's hatbox at Dover. If that grasping Skorsky had given me a proper contract I'd have made thousands.'

'Anarchism', said Artie, 'marijuana, pornography, ain't he devilish wicked? Someday, Edgar old son, you might even grow up.' He put down his sardine-tin, stood up and stretched himself. With his beard, sagging blue sweatshirt and paint-soiled jeans, he was a wild and formidable figure. 'Well, I guess I'll go now and hurl some paint at some canvas.' He turned to Dora. 'See you, bright eyes. So long, gentlemen.'

'You too, Edgar', said Dora. 'Henry and I want a quiet tête-à-tête dinner.'

'Very good, Lady Treffle', said Edgar. 'Call me if your new paramour proves tiresome. I shall now go to the U.S. Information Services Reading Room and steal some of their writing-paper. A small but concrete blow struck in the cause of the cold war.'

Their feet and swearing echoed down the wooden stairs.

'Really', said Henry, annoyed despite himself. 'I'm surprised you put up with the antics of those two ruffians.'

'I like them', Dora grinned wickedly at him, stretching her elegant satin-clad legs and sipping her cocktail. 'I like people who say exactly what they think, and do exactly what they want.' She refilled Henry's drink—he made a feeble attempt to stop her—perched gently on the arm of his chair and lowered her legs on to his knees. His throat contracted as he felt their silky warmth. She drew a crimson-crested index finger slowly down the side of his cheek.

'I can see you worry about me', she said softly. 'You shouldn't. I'm twenty-eight. I can take care of myself. Anyway I'm as common as dirt. I was brought up in a slum. I like lots of people around, warmth, noise, confusion, excitement. Those two boys aren't ruffians. They're like little children—little puppies—really. I don't mind them living here while I'm away. The *femme de ménage* will clear up their mess tomorrow. I like giving people things. If they want money, and I have some, I give it to them. I give people—other things—too. See?' She kissed him fiercely on the mouth, and he felt the slim, red snake of her tongue stealing hotly into his throat. He put his one unburdened arm—the other giddily held his drink—round her arched waist; the firm, excited muscles contracted under his touch.

She drew back her head, after what seemed to Henry like at least a minute and a half, and smiled down at him out of her smoky grey eyes. 'Great-hearted Dora', she said, 'that's me'.

'Some men', said Henry, with an immense attempt to collect his scattered mental faculties, 'do not like women who give everything—to everybody'.

Dora turned on him almost angrily. 'If you want to be happy in this place', she said, 'you must live and let live. I know nothing about the French, but I know that's the way they see life. It's a good way, too. Don't stand in judgement over other people, provided what they do

21

doesn't hurt others. That's the trouble with the English middle-class. I could feel you and Edgar judging each other, madly, just now—because, whatever Edgar says, he's just as bourgeois as you are. I'm not bourgeois. I'm a prole. I like people to be friendly and have fun.'

'You misunderstand me', said Henry desperately. 'I wasn't judging you. I like you. I was just saying that, for some men, women could be too indiscriminately generous'

'What makes you think I am? I said I liked giving. But there are things I wouldn't give to anyone—except perhaps Kiki.'

'Kiki?' asked Henry sharply. 'Who's Kiki?'

'I told you—my boy-friend in St. Tropez. Kiki's my pet name for him. He's a bit of a brute really, but I love him. He got rid of that odious Treffle boy for me, you see, and taught me that it's more important to be happy than famous. That sounds silly the way I put it, but it's *terribly* important to me. I'm a real existentialist now. Don't laugh. Perhaps I've had too many drinks, but I see it very clearly—why I love Kiki. I think perhaps I *would* give him anything.'

'Except fidelity', said Henry a little sourly. Kiki was beginning to dominate the conversation too much for his liking. 'Would Kiki like to see us two here now?'

'No. Yes. I don't think he'd mind. That's a mean question. It's one you shouldn't ask a woman. Kiki has his girls, I know; I don't really mind them, so long as they're not around when we're together. I don't think he minds me being with men either, so long as he's not there. When he is, the men *aren't* around. Simple, isn't it?'

She finished her drink. The tension, and with it the atmosphere of a few moments before, seemed to be broken. 'Let's go and have dinner', she said.

They dined on the other side of the Boulevard, at Chez Artur on the Rue Giselle. Henry's stomach felt distended with emotion, and he had little appetite, despite his meagre lunch; he now felt so immersed in a remorseless chain of events which would lead either to the attainment of this woman, or to some unforeseen catastrophe which would snatch her from him in the moment of fulfilment, that food seemed not merely irrelevant but an irritating interruption. But Dora ate heartily; and by the time she had consumed *pâté de canard en croûte* and an *escalope Holstein*, and drunk three or four glasses of Pouilly Fuissé, her reckless good humour had returned. She was also unmistakably, if slightly, drunk. She told Henry about her early life in Stepney; about how her mother had saved up for her to have ballet lessons; about dancing as a child-fairy in pantomimes; about her first West End show in the chorus; about how she met Fanshaw Treffle in a night club; about their elopement, marriage, quarrels and final disaster. As she told it, it was quite a funny story, but pathetic too, and Henry felt himself warming to her. As he gazed into her laughing, childish eyes, felt the unsubtle pressure of her knee against his, and the touch of her warm hand on his thigh, he found himself liking as well as wanting her.

As he paid the bill, she said: 'I was going to suggest we go to the Café Zok to meet the gang. But now I want to go home quick. I want you to make love to me before I get too sleepy.'

This was absolutely the right remark for her to make, thought Henry; entirely characteristic, direct and amoral. But, while quite determined to go to bed with Dora, certain, now, that he was at last to acquire a fully-fledged mistress, he was quite unsure of the reply he ought to

23

make. Indeed, he felt that all along he had failed at any point to wrench the initiative from Dora, but had remained simply a lay figure, leaving her to position his inanimate limbs in accordance with her whims or desires. But then what *did* one say when an incredibly desirable young woman asked one to sleep with her? The thing was not merely unprecedented in his experience, it was unforeseeable. He contented himself with nodding, and clumsily pressing her arm.

When they stood inside the door of her flat, Dora kissed him again, pressing her tight, full body against his: the coat of his London suit was open, and he felt the hard peaks of her nipples through his shirt. He began to insert an exploratory hand under her blouse.

'Naughty', said Dora, her cockney twang, which had grown that evening with every drink, now uppermost in her voice. 'Don't be so impatient, pretty boy. Dora's had a hard couple of days. Dora wants to take a shower and freshen up a little. You stay in the studio like a good little boy, and give yourself a drink while Dora gets ready.'

The bathroom and Dora's bedroom opened off the studio. Through the half-open door, Henry presently heard the sound of splashing water. He went to the array of bottles on the table and mixed himself a large brandy-and-soda. As he sipped it, an immense glow of self-confidence began to well up inside him. For the first time his apprehensions about the affair began to subside. He acknowledged to himself, happily, a sense of possession, not only of Dora, but of this squalidly glamorous apartment, through whose window the lights of Paris gleamed mistily. He was a man waiting for his mistress to take a shower before she took him to her arms. This was *really* what he had come to Paris for, and Racine could go to hell. He took a large gulp of his drink, and wandered happily about the studio. Dora's taste—or was it Kiki's (the thought of him did not disturb Henry's complacency; *he* was the man in possession now)—seemed extraordinarily mixed. One of the armchairs was evidently a fine Louis Quinze *bergère*, the other unmistakably a French, and infinitely worse, version of Tottenham Court Road. Besides the *tâchiste* paintings on the walls, which the art critic of the *Observer* had persuaded Henry to approve, but which he secretly rather disliked, were Medici prints, old steel engravings—perhaps they belonged to the landlord?—and etchings by Daumier.

The books were a mixed lot, too. Henry poured himself another drink and began to delve among them. Here was Sartre's *La Nausée*. No doubt the existentialist-teaching Kiki was responsible for that. And an odd volume of Lenin's *Collected Works*: Edgar, this time, without a doubt. *Peyton Place*, *The Naked and the Dead*, Ian Fleming's *Doctor No*— these were clearly Dora's, just the sort of books she would read. And here, incongruously, were the *Poetical Works* of William Wordsworth. Who could that belong to? Wordsworth was scarcely the type of poet Edgar would admire, let alone read. Henry opened the cover and saw the coat-of-arms of Cranpole School. Most extraordinary. Henry had been at Cranpole too. Who could have stolen it from the school library and eventually deposited it in Dora's Left Bank love-nest? The only person Henry could possibly think of was an odious man called Michael Crick, who had bullied him at school and later condescended to him at Oxford, where he had been three or four steps ahead of Henry in worldly wisdom. Crick had reputedly seduced one of the school chambermaids, and at Oxford, where he had kept a succession of enviable mistresses, had given Henry an occasional piece of gratuitous—and deeply resented—advice on how to make women. Crick was certainly capable of stealing books from the school library and also of leaving them in Left Bank flats. But he had been sent down in Henry's first year and later, so Henry had heard, been arrested in Singapore and imprisoned for fraud. The book had probably been left by an earlier generation of Cranpolean philanderers; it was certainly old enough.

Still musing on this problem, Henry poured himself another large drink. He was one up on Crick now. While Crick, deservedly, rotted in some Oriental gaol, he was lolling at his ease in his mistress's apartment. Or rather, he corrected himself, his imminent mistress. And what, come to that, was Dora doing? Henry looked at his watch, squinting furiously. Eleven-thirty. He listened. No sound came from the bathroom, and she had been gone over half an hour. Was she performing some mysterious, feminine and silent rite, into which he should not intrude? Or perhaps she was simply waiting for him, her lord and master, to come and take his pleasure. Much more likely; and, being Dora, she was probably growing impatient. He had better investigate.

Henry rose to his feet and walked unsteadily towards Dora's bedroom. For the first time he became dimly conscious that he had had too much to drink. This did not dismay him in the least; drink and sex, he told himself, were the great inseparables, like Fortnum and Mason, Marx and Engels, Auden and Isherwood. 'That which hath made them drunk hath made me bold', he quoted complacently, pushing open the door.

The room was pink. Pink satin curtains, pink bedspread, a deep crimson carpet, and a pink bedside lamp which radiated pink light over Dora's pink and plushy body. She lay stretched out on the bed, on her stomach, fast asleep. On her face, which lay turned towards the door, was an expression of childish contentment. Except for a single bangle round her wrist, she was stark naked, and Henry found his gaze straying to her round and rosy bottom, which rose and fell gently to the rhythm of her breathing.

What to do? Henry pondered slowly in the doorway. Had he been an older, more experienced man, he would have had no doubts. But he was not an experienced man. He was, moreover, drunk. 'That which hath made them drunk hath made me bold', he repeated. So far, he reminded himself, Dora had made all the moves in this game. She had retained the sexual initiative throughout. Now it was his turn to wrest it back. He dimly remembered the odious Crick saying in his superior way, 'There's nothing more calculated, old man, to excite a woman than a good hard slap on her behind. None of your playful taps, mind. A real stinger. They come up foaming at the mouth'. And Crick, though awful and criminal, undoubtedly knew about women. Dora's bottom invited him. Here was his chance, at one blow, to reassume his masculine, paramount role in their relationship. Draining his glass, and setting it down decisively on the dressing-table, he advanced purposefully over Dora's sleeping form and brought his hand down with tremendous force.

The effect was cataclysmic. In one galvanic movement, Dora leapt to her feet and turned to face him, the dreamy contentment on her face replaced by glaring anger.

27

'You ——', she screamed, her face stretched with animal rage. 'You stinking little ——.'

'I say', exclaimed Henry, 'that was meant to be friendly, you know.'

'Well it hurt, you little pig. And I was having a blissful dream. So now you can get out. Quick.' She pointed brusquely to the door. 'Go on, move.'

'But look here', said Henry nervously, still hovering in the door. She turned round to the bedside table, seized a large porcelain ashtray, and hurled it venomously at his head. It bounded off the doorpost and fell with a crash to the floor. Henry retreated. 'Please let me explain', he protested desperately.

'Get out', she repeated menacingly, and began to look for other missiles. Henry dodged into the hall, turned and called out appealingly: 'I'll telephone you to explain.'

A book came hurling through the air. 'Telephone my ——', called out Dora's voice stridently. 'I never want to see your snot-nosed prissy face again. *And get out.*'

It had all happened so swiftly that Henry had had no time to marshal even his drink-befuddled thoughts before he was out on the street. Somehow or other, the crystal chalice had been dashed from his lips just as he was about to sip. He had made a mistake, clearly, but it had not been entirely his fault. Dora was like all other women, promising more than she would fulfil. She had presented him with an image of herself which was false, which he had accepted at its face value, and which had shattered immediately he had tried to grasp at it. In a way, he was not surprised. He had never quite believed in the thing anyway. It had all been too good to be true.

Thus brooding, he returned to his hotel. Madame Marcourt, who was still presiding over the desk, gave

28

him a cordial goodnight. 'I trust it was successful, your first evening in Paris?' she intoned. Henry grunted and began to stumble slowly up the stairs. An eventful evening, anyway. But it had settled one thing: the *Cours de Civilisation* not only ought to come first in his life, it clearly *was* going to come first. Dora was a dead loss now; and this was, unequivocally, a good thing. But his new mattress felt very hard, cold and lonely, all the same; and it was some time before he fell into a troubled and drunken sleep.

# II

HENRY awoke in suicidal mood. He had a bad hang-over. He discovered, on going through his pockets, that he had spent 6,000 francs the day before—almost his ration for a whole week. Worst of all, he realized he had made a complete ass of himself; for, having first of all decided to avoid entangling himself with Dora in order to pursue his *Cours de Civilisation*, he had not only abandoned his vow at the first breath of temptation, but had failed to justify—even at the lowest level—his moral weakness by deriving any profane satisfaction from it. He was that most pathetic and ridiculous figure of all—the unsuccessful sinner. The only consolation, and this a slender one, was that he had learnt his lesson early. He had tasted the forbidden fruits of Paris and found them turn to ashes in his mouth. The experience might well prove to be cheap at the price, and at any rate his future course was now unmistakably clear: the sober life beckoned him, not merely on moral grounds, but on grounds of sheer expediency. Henry, however, was not entirely convinced by this argument. For a young man of liberal education, pronounced views and adequate self-esteem, he had surprisingly little faith in his ability to avoid disaster.

His watch told him it was already nine o'clock, and his first lecture was at ten. Henry dressed rapidly, discarding his London suit in favour of sports jacket and flannels, and hurried down to the Boulevard for breakfast. But the thought of food appalled him, and he ordered a glass of Vichy water; a fine beginning, he told himself bitterly, for his first day of devotion to French civilization. He forced himself dutifully to read *Le Figaro*, plunging into the labyrinth of French politics. M. Felix Gaillard, said the headline, was running grave risks in the coming debate on Algeria. *Le Figaro's* political correspondent was concerned by the attitude likely to be adopted by numerous groups, notably the Dissident-Gaullists, the Independent-Peasants, and what he termed 'a far from negligible minority of the Radicals'. Owing to the obscurities of the government's own position on the matter, other deputies had failed to declare their voting intentions, and it had proved impossible to take a *pointage*. There would, it was already clear, be a battle of orders of the day, and much would depend on whether M. Gaillard was prepared to promise a rise in ex-servicemen's pensions, an increase in the subsidies to beetroot-growers, distillers and wine-farmers, and the award of danger-money to the police, whose current mood, according to *Le Figaro*, was *sceptique sinon ambigue*. His greatest safeguard, the article concluded, was the total failure, so far, to find even a limited measure of agreement as to his successor.

Having done his political homework, Henry set out for the Sorbonne, walking along the Boulevard St. Germain and up the Boulevard St. Michel. There seemed to be a great many young men about, muttering and arguing in groups; and even more policemen, looking *sceptique* perhaps, but certainly far from *ambigue*—indeed, positively hostile. Clearly, some people were prepared to take French politics seriously, thought Henry, with the detached condescension English liberals reserve for fanatical and incomprehensible Continentals. Some of the young men

31

carried placards reading *Jeune Nation—Algérie Française*.
Others carried banners: *Les Fascistes ne passeront pas*.

At the crossroads where the two boulevards meet, the
inevitable happened. A solid phalanx of Communists,
who appeared to be acting as escort to an elderly gentleman selling *L'Humanité*, marched directly into the advance line of a group of *Jeune Nation* youths. Neither
seemed willing to give way, and Henry, from the other
side of the boulevard, watched the mobs converge on
each other with the majestic stateliness of two armadas
joining battle. When twenty paces apart, both sides broke
into a run, the Communists joining together the poles of
their principal banner for use as a battering ram. The
clash was glorious while it lasted. The ram struck a
portly Fascist directly in the stomach and bowled him
over, then careered dizzily through the window of a
chocolate shop; marzipan bars and *petits-fours* rained on
to the pavement. A dozen individual fights broke out,
both sides using their feet as well as fists, in what Henry
regarded as a most unsportsmanlike manner. The old
newspaper-seller, deserted by his guards, was knocked
down and his newspapers scattered over the street.

Then came the cry: *Les Flics!* Henry turned and saw
a formidable army of Riot Police, wearing steel-helmets
and swinging massive white truncheons, advancing up
the Boulevard St. Germain; behind them trundled a
convoy of Black Marias. The Communists—who num-
bered less than fifty—began to retreat instantly towards
the Place St. Michel; the Fascists, after a half-hearted
cry of '*La Police avec Nous*' (there seemed to be a stereo-
typed vocabulary for each phase in the ballet, Henry
noted) followed suit. The police quickened their pace
to a trot, and within a few seconds the corner of the

32

boulevard was deserted, except for a few dazed youths sitting or lying on the pavement. The police advanced on them remorselessly. Two policemen seized the first, dragged him to his feet, and held him while a third beat him systematically about the head and shoulders with his truncheon; then he was dragged off unconscious to a Black Maria. The second figure they pounced on was the old newspaper-seller, who was painfully scrabbling about on the ground collecting his papers. Again two police-men seized him; again a third prepared to set about him with his stick.

At this point, Henry, who had been watching the scene with growing horror—the comic-opera ballet had suddenly transformed itself into bleeding tragedy—decided to intervene, with all the authority of an indig-nant English sportsman preventing foreigners from making beasts of themselves.

'Stop it!' he shouted from across the road. '*Arrêtez-vous!*'

The two policemen who were holding the old man looked up, astonished. The third turned round, regarded Henry with a mixture of bewilderment and annoyance, and then began to advance towards him. For the first time, a feeling of personal unease crept over Henry. He became aware that he was the only spectator who had remained in the street; though countless interested eyes watched from behind windows, shutters and shop-fronts.

'Come here, you', shouted the advancing policeman, pointing his truncheon at Henry. Henry hesitated. As an observer of this disgraceful scene, it was clearly his duty to complain to the police. But from the behaviour of the policeman—which in this case was extremely *ambigue*, to put it mildly—it seemed unlikely that his

33

complaint would be well received. Perhaps the man believed he had been taking part in the scrimmage—a not unreasonable conclusion since he was apparently the only spectator. And Henry had a distinct recollection that there were fierce laws in France for dealing with foreigners who participated in domestic politics.

Henry turned and began to walk towards the Place St. Michel.

'Stop!' said the policeman, and began to run. Henry found himself running too. To run seemed the obvious thing, even though it meant a retreat from clearly defined principles, for the policeman was obviously not going to listen to reason. Henry had no wish to be hit on the head with a truncheon before he had had time to make his point, however unanswerable.

Henry had never been chased by a policeman before, and was disagreeably surprised by the turn of speed shown by this one, despite the handicap of his formidable equipment. He dodged back down the Boulevard, with the man pounding along twenty yards behind, then plunged into the labyrinth of side streets behind the Quai St. Michel. It might have been extremely embarrassing to identify oneself thus openly as a criminal pursued by the law, if Henry had had time to think about it. But he was now beyond such nuances of discomfort, being conscious not only of his pounding lungs—he had not run so fast since taking the assault-course at a War Office Selection Board—but of a growing realization that he was going to be caught. The policeman was clearly gaining, and by deciding to run in the first place, Henry had virtually admitted his guilt; it would be held in evidence against him.

Henry lurched desperately into a dark and narrow

34

street, which ran like a canyon between high walls of crumbling houses. Suddenly, the pursuing footsteps ceased. Henry turned round, and saw the policeman lying on the floor, with two youths belabouring him with his own truncheon. There was no-one else about. Henry hurried back to the struggling group, but by the time he reached them, the policeman, whose helmet had been removed, and whose face was now covered in blood, was unconscious. The two young men stood up smiling and gave Henry the Communist salute.

'Welcome, Comrade', said one of them—a tall, fair-haired boy of about twenty, wearing an elegant tweed jacket over faultlessly-pressed dark grey flannels. 'We are delighted to come to your assistance and dispose of this capitalist lackey.' He held out his hand. 'My name is Pierre-Emile Jeansson, student of law, and this is Edouard le Gros, student of architecture.' He indicated his plump, cherubic companion, who was dressed in orthodox Left Bank sweater and jeans. Henry identified him as Number One on the banner battering-ram.

Still breathless, he shook hands. 'I'm most grateful', he said, marshalling his remaining French, 'but I do hope you haven't killed the wretched man.'

'Ah! I see you are a foreigner', exlaimed Pierre-Emile. 'English perhaps? I thought so. Do not break your head about this miserable *flic*. We have merely given him a taste of his own medicine. He will doubtless recover in a day or so, and in future, I trust, think twice about attacking peaceful English gentlemen. And now, I fear, we must all retreat. Our poor *flic* may be missed by his colleagues. Won't you join us in a cup of coffee?'

Leaving the recumbent policeman, all three marched smartly down to the Quai, turned left and entered the small student café at the bottom of the Rue Bonaparte. There was no sign of any police, and Henry gathered they were now safe.

'There are rules to this game', explained Pierre-Emile. 'If they catch you on the spot, you've had it: a sharp taste of their *bâtons* and a day in the cells. But if you break clean away, they don't bother to pursue you very far. The incident is now over.'

'But it's dangerous', said Henry heatedly. 'The police appear to be quite indiscriminate about who they attack. was merely a spectator, and attempted to come to the rescue of an old man they were beating up. Then they turned on *me*!'

The two Frenchmen exchanged glances and laughed. 'My dear friend', said Pierre-Emile, 'You are not in London now. This is France, a country where the class-war is still waged fiercely and where the police exist to defend the privileges of the bourgeoisie. There is none of your gentle little parliamentary game here. In Paris, we play politics, as you say, for keeps. You see this'—he pulled back a lock of hair which fell over his forehead, revealing an inch-long angry red scar—'I got it just before Christmas, in the course of an exchange of views with *Jeune Nation*. This country is approaching a crisis, and it is not going to be solved within the Chamber, I can tell you. The Fascists are arming, both here, and even more so in Algiers, where they practically run the army and administration. We Communists are arming too, though we are not so strong as a few years ago. Still, we will put up a fight. When the pathetic Gaillard ministry falls—as it will, soon—then everything will start: you will see. Is this not true, Edouard?'

'Yes', said Edouard. 'Listen. I know there is a group of

people in *Jeune Nation* who are actively planning a *coup d'état*. They are in touch with a senior deputy, and also with certain army officers in Algiers—the parachute commanders you know. I do not know the name of the deputy though I have my suspicions. But at a given signal—and it will come during the next *crise*—they will strike simultaneously. The deputy has powerful friends among the army command here—he has held important office, you see. They will allow the *Jeune Nation* shock-troops to take over one of the airfields near Paris—Villecouvray, perhaps—and then the paras will be landed. They will bring back De Gaulle as their front-man, and set up a Fascist dictatorship.'

'But this is simply frightful', said Henry. 'If it's true, why isn't it published in the papers? If people in the government know about it, why don't they arrest the army commanders?'

Again the two students laughed. 'This is France', said Pierre-Emile. 'The ministers cannot get their orders obeyed in Algiers already. If they instructed General Salan, who commands in Algeria, to arrest these para colonels, he would resign, and then the revolt would start. Besides, many ministers are hedging their bets. They do not know what will happen, and they want to be on the winning side. They are afraid for their jobs, their parliamentary seats, their mistresses, their bank-accounts. And the newspapers? Only *L'Humanité* and *Libération* have attempted to tell the truth. And they are seized by the police. The others—even the liberal ones—are too scared. Everyone is scared in France to-day.'

'But will people put up with it?' asked Henry.

'The people are apathetic. They are living well—better than ever before. They want a quiet life and their prosperity to continue. They are sick of the Fourth Republic and its politicians. They do not care what takes its place so long as they are left alone. That is why I am a Communist. The people must be alerted, and only the Communist Party has the courage to do it.'

'Now look here', said Henry, 'I can't accept that. What about Hungary and all that? And the Berlin riots? Communism is practically the same as Fascism, isn't it? I can't think of one of my friends who's Communist, I must confess. I had some hopes that the Russians might behave in a more reasonable way after Mr. Krushchev's speech at the Twentieth Party Congress—a paper I take published it in full, and I conscientiously read every word—but that phase seems to have come to an end. I don't think a democrat could possibly support them to-day.'

'Listen', said Pierre-Emile impatiently. 'I keep telling you this is France, not England. We have no social democracy here, we have no nice Mr. Gaitskells and Bevans and Labour Parties. Mollet and the Socialists are in league with the bourgeoisie and the army. Look at what happened after the last election. Mollet promised to make peace in Algeria, and immediately he got into power he turned a somersault and carried on the war worse than before. Mendès-France is finished, and anyway he was responsible for the re-arming of Germany. That leaves only the C.P. What happens in Hungary or elsewhere is not our immediate business. I could elaborate a defence for it in Marxist terms, but it would bore you and doubtless leave you unconvinced. What concerns me is what is going to happen *here*, in France. Right here, Communism is our only defence against Fascism because it is the only political instrument which can mobilize the workers.'

'As an Englishman', added Edouard, 'you do not understand the psychology of the French left. There is no place for Social Democrats in our political spectrum. The radical Frenchman inherits the traditions of the Revolution and the barricades. He thinks in these terms. He is impatient with gradualist solutions. When he votes left, he automatically votes for the extreme left, for the Communist Party is the only political embodiment of the Revolutionary tradition. He is not a Marxist. He is not voting primarily for Communism. He is voting for *change*—immediate, total and transcendental change. Do you understand?'

'Well of course I understand *that*', said Henry, 'though I can't believe it's the best way to set about it. I've always believed that violent change was in itself undesirable, and in any case usually produces an equally violent reaction. Your motives in working for the Communist Party are doubtless admirable, but surely you're aware that its direction is completely in the hands of men who get their orders from Moscow.'

'Of course we know that', said Pierre-Emile angrily. 'We hear it every day in *Le Figaro*. I get it from my father, who owns a big department store, each time I dine at home. It may even be true. But what does it matter? We have to take first things first. Our immediate problem is to save the Republic. We can decide what happens afterwards when the time comes. Thorez and Duclos are the old gang—we shall get them out somehow. But would you have us spend all our time and energy doing that, while the Fascists are taking over France?'

'No', said Henry dubiously. 'I don't know that I can answer your question.' He caught sight of the clock over the bar of the café: it was ten past ten. 'And look here, I

39

must go to my lecture. I'm already ten minutes late.'

'Lecture?' said Pierre-Emile. 'What lecture?'

'I'm taking a course in French civilization at the Sorbonne.'

They laughed. 'This *is* French civilization', said Pierre-Emile. 'That's what we're talking about—how to save it. At the moment, we haven't got any time to waste on *studying* it.'

'I'm sorry', said Henry apologetically. 'But it's my first day on the course and I simply must go. We can carry on our conversation another time—though I know you won't convince me.'

'Good', said Pierre-Emile, rising and holding out his hand. 'And we must get back to the task of perfecting our organization. You can find us in this café most mornings. And we are usually at the *Deux Magots* before dinner. See you on the barricades!'

'*A bientôt!*' said Edouard.

Henry hurried to the Sorbonne, carefully avoiding the Boulevard St. Michel, where he feared the police might still be out in force. Around the entrance to the Sorbonne, a good many students were gathered, still discussing the incident. But he was safe here: the police kept their distance from the university, though several Black Marias could be seen parked in the surrounding streets. There was a good audience for the Racine lecture: Americans mostly—more than half of them girls—quite a few Dutch and Scandinavians, and a sprinkling of English. Henry crept in and took a seat in the back row behind a pair of young American girls. The lecturer droned on; from where Henry sat it was impossible to distinguish anything of what he was saying. In any case, the girls in front were chattering noisily.

'My director of studies at Stanhope insists I get my card stamped for each lecture I attend. Now that's what I call un-American.'

'Honey, the way I see it, we might just as well be here listening to this old goat. I don't know a single boy who gets up before lunch.'

'Did that dreamy Michel date you? *You* know, the one whose father is a count.'

'I'll say. His father may be a count—though I think a lot of these French beaux are phonies—but Michel is certainly no gentleman. He asked me up to his room in the Hotel Aiglon, to show me his mother's jewels, *he* said. I was no sooner in the door than he simply *pounced*, tearing at my Saks sweater like a sort of *bear*. No build-up, nothing. An absolute Commie. I had to fight, I can tell you, and I've got bruises to show, too. I haven't come across such a direct approach since my first high school Commem.'

'You going to date him again?'

'Natch—I mean, naturally. As you correctly observed, Angie *dear*, he's dreamy. But I gave it to him straight. See here, monsieur, I said—in French too—if you want to make me, you'll have to exercise a little more of that old southern European charm of yours. I'm not a fraulein from Stockholm, I said. Where's that romantic *parlez-vous*, I said. You'd better produce some of it, friend, if you want to get your hand up *my* skirt. Hell, what am I in France *for*?'

The abrupt translation from Marxist dialectic to college dormitory gossip—coupled with his lingering hang-over—was too much for Henry. He moved round to the other side of the lecture-hall, a grey, echoing building, its seats built on tiers like a football grandstand. Henry

41

wedged himself in the back row, his feet against the row in front, and closed his eyes wearily. But again, conversation, mostly in English, drifted up.

'I believe that hag who owns the Zok was what they call a *collabo*—you know, worked with the Germans during the war. Slept with Goering or somebody. Come the Liberation, they shaved all her hair off and turned her loose in the Rue Radiguet stark naked.'

'Spare me the image, son. That Goering had some taste.'

'Sure, he liked 'em strong and meaty.'

'Apropos of meat, you seen that Austrian girl who sings calypsos at the Bar Medici? Now that's what I call a nice piece of ass.'

'Sure, I've seen her. She's a junky. Shacks up with a great buck nigger from Florida. Watch your step there, Hadley. That piece is marked *Propriété Privée: Défence d'Entrer*. That big buck had a disputation with Art Scholfurst at a party last fall and pulled a knife on him.'

'Excuse my interrupting your conversation, but do you mind not using pejorative terms like nigger and buck? Some of us have come here to study civilization, you know. And might I take the opportunity to point out to you, since you are both clearly Americans, that it is precisely your lack of consideration for coloured races which is losing your country the Cold War. Now we in Ceylon, for instance. . . .'

'. . . so if I'm seen with this French boy, how do I know he's not a Communist? I'm a liberal myself, Adlai Stevenson's reactionary so far as I'm concerned, but I have to think of my passport. Now I happen to know that the passport bureau at the Consulate employ several of these Left Bank bums to report on us. They see you with a

French Communist, and when your passport comes up for renewal the clerk says "Nothing doing, sister", and you're back in the States. . . .'

'. . . take, if I may be permitted to give you an example, the refusal to supply arms to the peace-loving state of Indonesia. My people took this as a calculated insult to the Afro-Asian bloc. . . .'

'. . . after all, it shouldn't be goddam necessary to plead the Fifth Amendment on your sex-life. . . .'

'. . . sixty-thousand francs she cost me, old boy, one way or another. . . .'

'. . . as Jaharawal Nehru has put it. . . .'

'. . . would I pose for him, he ask. You have fine figure, he say. Show me paint, canvas, studio first, I say. Then I know you painter. He say, he go buy 'em. No sale, I say. Fine figure, hell, I say. I know your sort, I say. . . .'

'Shut up!' said Henry loudly and fiercely. Sex and politics—could nobody talk about anything else in this city? His exasperation conveyed itself effectively to the back rows. There was a sudden silence. The lecturer, aware that something was wrong, ceased to mutter and glanced up. His eye rested on the clock, which stood at a minute past eleven. With unconcealed pleasure, he gathered up his notes and left the room. Casting suspicious and reproachful glances at Henry, the class broke up.

Henry lunched alone near the Panthéon, nibbling a hard, dry ham sandwich, and probing dutifully through the columns of *Le Monde*. Jacques Fauvet, the paper's political correspondent, seemed even less certain of the future shape of events than his colleague on *Le Figaro*, but agreed that M. Gaillard's prospects were daily diminishing. He also wrote of 'a certain effervescence'

43

among students on the Left Bank that morning, but there was no mention of a dead policeman, so Henry assumed that his pursuer had recovered. That was good from one point of view; on the other hand, the policeman would shortly be round and about, and might conceivably recognize him. He would have to be careful.

Henry trudged over to the Luxembourg Gardens. His hangover was wearing off now, and he filled his lungs gratefully with the clean spring air. The park was crowded with children, nannies, mothers; dozens of sailing-boats bobbed on the pond. This was the Paris of Colette and the young Proust, domestic, bourgeois and safe. Tiny girls, in prim, crisp linen frocks and long black stockings, raced by, spinning plastic windmills on sticks. There were stalls selling toffee-apples and liquorice, paper masks and huge cornets of pink sugar-wool. And picture post-cards. Henry remembered he had not written home yet. He selected a garish colour-photograph of the Eiffel Tower (there were no art-reproductions) addressed it to his mother, and wrote on the back:'Arrived safely. Everything marvellous. Hotel v. comfortable and have already met many interesting new friends. Attended excellent lecture on Racine's sense of tragedy this morning. Will write at length soon. Love to you and father, H.'

The bench on which Henry sat was already warm with sunshine—it was a hot afternoon for March—and within five minutes he was asleep. He dreamt he was addressing the National Assembly from the back bench of the lecture hall at the Sorbonne; for reasons which were obscure, Dora's life was on trial and he was making an impassioned plea on her behalf. Murmurs of dissent interrupted his speech, and as his peroration concluded and he sat down, the assembled deputies, wearing steel helmets, rose up and clambered towards him over the benches, flourishing truncheons and Fascist slogans. Henry woke up trembling with cold; it was already half-past six, the children had gone, the sun was low on the horizon, and the evening was clear and chilly.

The first day of Henry's assault on French civilization was now entirely spent, with nothing to show for it, at any rate in the line of academic education. On the other hand, his hangover had disappeared, and the evening was young. Henry left the Luxembourg, walked down the Rue de Tournon, crossed the Boulevard and plunged into the Marché St. Germain, which was thronged with housewives, students and assorted Left-Bankers buying their dinners. The Marché stands at the head of the Rue de Seine which, Henry knew, was crowded with tiny and obscure art galleries, containing all that was new and outrageous in French painting. Their exploration was clearly one of the aspects of Paris life he should cover, and would compensate, at least in part, for his dissipations.

The first gallery contained paintings of red-and-blue rhomboids, with pink excrescences, signed Krob. Henry had been taught that the way to appreciate modern paintings was to identify the outstanding characteristics of each canvas and to examine the way in which they contributed to what the artist was trying to say, or, if this was indecipherable, to the 'total conception'. Krob's total conception, he decided, was the rhomboids. They seemed rather clumsy and uncouth, denoting therefore strength and stability rather than dynamism or grace. The pink excrescences added lightness, indicating that life was not quite so simple as one might think at first

45

glance. Henry noticed that the paint of the rhomboids was thick; this was clearly deliberate—Krob had wished to add a third dimension to reinforce the solidity of his rhomboids. Henry now felt he had mastered Krob: since the degree of apparent skill in each of his canvases was roughly equal, the best was the one which had (*a*) the thickest paint on the rhomboids; (*b*) the most excrescences—especially where they were a very light shade of pink. He picked the canvas which conformed to this analysis and, being a practical-minded person at heart, asked the bored gallery assistant behind the desk which he thought was the best painting in the show.

'That one, monsieur', said the attendant, indicating the canvas Henry had chosen.

Henry was jubilant. 'And is it the most expensive?'

'Naturally'.

His theory of modern art triumphantly vindicated, Henry left the gallery and collided heavily with a bearded man carrying an immense and bedraggled portfolio. It was Artie, the American he had met the previous evening at Dora's.

Henry was delighted to see him, and immediately explained how he had got to the bottom of Krob, and how his choice had been confirmed by the authority of the market.

Artie laughed. 'You know the real reason why that canvas is priced up? Because it's the largest. Look at it again: it's at least one square foot bigger than any of the others. Painters like Krob—and that includes most of them—sell strictly by size.'

'I can't believe it. If it were true, everyone would be painting enormous murals forty-foot long.'

'No—because the system works only up to a point. It's

46

just like selling automobiles: there's an optimum size. Little ones are cheap, because the art-buying classes have large apartments, and they don't want their trophies buried. On the other hand, modern apartments seldom have ceilings more than twelve feet high and people like the focal-point of the painting to be just above eye-level, so they can look at them from the cocktail tray. All right. Granted that people still believe in the Golden Section, which means a rough five-to-three ratio in breadth and depth, your optimum-sized painting is about two-and-a-half feet broad by one-and-a-half high, excluding frame. See? And now let's go have a drink.'

Artie took him to a workers' bar farther up the street, where wine was sold from the barrel at fifteen francs a glass.

'Of course', he said, 'there are exceptions. Once your reputation gets beyond a certain point, you can afford to paint big from time to time, because you're in what I call the hand-out class. All the hand-out institutions—Rockefeller, Ford, Unesco, government agencies, public galleries, trades union headquarters—they have big walls they've got to cover somehow. They buy paintings by the square yard. They're not interested in quality, just quantity. Why, they even supply you with free paint and canvas, so long as you cover it. I occasionally try my hand at one of the big ones, so I'm ready for when I hit the jackpot.'

'This is absurd', said Henry. 'The worst kind of transatlantic cynicism, if I may say so. A painter can't simply conform to arbitrary limitations of size, laid down by fashion. It isn't art.'

'What's art got to do with it? This is the mid-twentieth century, boy. Nobody knows anything about art any more. There aren't any standards or criteria of what's good. About fifty years ago, Cézanne and the Fauves discovered a technique for painting pictures without revealing they had any talent. They had, of course, but they took it for granted and went beyond it. Well, the technique caught on. You got Cubism, Expressionism, Surrealism and all the other isms down to *tâchisme* and Action Painting. Gradually, painters began to realize that they didn't have to have any talent to make a hit: all that was needed was a gimmick. If you—and your agents—plugged the gimmick hard enough, you caught on.'

'But most modern painters can draw superbly if they choose, or so we're always being told. And they learn the academic techniques at the art schools.'

'Sure. But it isn't so simple as that. The impression has got around that all a painter has to do is to spend three years drawing plaster casts and then he has his technique all lined up. He sort of graduates, and afterwards he can forget all about skill and concentrate on his gimmick. It isn't true. Learning to paint is a twenty-four hour, lifetime job. But hardly anybody does it nowadays. Why should they? Why take the hard way, when you can get rich *and* send the experts the easy way? Modern art has been big money for over a generation now. The result is, nobody knows anything about painting any more.'

Henry ordered two more *coups de vin rouge*. 'Are you maintaining', he asked, 'that there is no real difference in quality between individual modern painters? That it's all an enormous confidence trick?'

'Not exactly. It's an extraordinary example of high-pressure public relations at its most futile. Now that there are no longer any objective standards of quality, nobody really knows what makes a good painting, least of all the painters themselves. Theoretically, public relations is the art of selling a good product to the public—it's part of the educational process. In the field of painting, it should work as follows. A painter creates a new type of image. It's good. The critics single him out. The galleries take him up and sell him to the public. But in practice, it doesn't work like that. Since painting has ceased to be a craft, the painter is working in the dark. He doesn't know when his work is good, because he doesn't know what "good" is. Nor do the critics, whose business is to acclaim good work when they see it, not to tell the painter how to create it. That throws the onus of choice on the galleries. But the gallery owners are simply businessmen. If they are given a good product to sell, they will sell it. But if they are asked to select the product themselves, they naturally pick one they think the public will want. So the choice is ultimately thrust on the public, which is the most bewildered section of all. That way, nobody ever gets any wiser: they spin around in a vicious circle of invincible ignorance.'

'But this is a fantastically gloomy view. If you really believe it, why do you remain a painter yourself?'

'Because I think the vicious circle is going to be broken —perhaps quite soon—and then the entire superstructure will collapse. You can fool the public about anything for one generation, but not for two. Modern art's had a good run for its money, but its number's up now. The crash would have come already if the big wheels of the art world weren't so deeply committed. Besides, once the process starts, where will it end? If *tâchisme* is exposed as rubbish, people will start asking questions about other isms. The Russians found this out in 1956. They thought it was O.K. to denounce Stalin and leave it at that. But then the moujiks began to have doubts about Lenin, too, and so on right back to Papa Marx. If Jackson Pollock's no good, how long can Picasso remain on his pedestal? Or Chagall or Matisse or Gauguin or Van Gogh, and so on right back to the greatest "genius" of all, Cézanne? Where do you draw the line? The answer is you can't. That's why the Stalinists of the art world will fight tooth and nail against the least hint of revisionism.'

'Go on', said Henry, 'I'm beginning to be impressed. If there's no crack in the Stalinist ranks, who's going to start the counter-revolution?'

'I'm coming to that, boy.' Artie drained his glass and ordered another round. 'I'll tell you who's going to start it—us, the painters. We're growing sick and tired and disgusted with the whole thing. What makes a man want to become a painter—which isn't much of a job, anyway? Because he likes to create something beautiful. But nowadays he's asked to hurl pots of paint at a canvas, and then roll in the muck. He doesn't like doing it. He wants to get back to the fine line, the delicate tone, the infinite shade of colour, the exactitude of composition, all the million subtleties which make painting the highest expression of human genius. This feeling has been building up for some time. I expect that *tâchisme* will prove to be the last straw. Its sheer, goddamn ridiculousness may touch off the explosion. And then you and I, boy, will be able to sit back and watch the whole rotten superstructure of modern art come crashing down in ruins. In twenty years' time, second-hand shops will be offering Picassos for a hundred dollars—and there won't be any takers. We'll live to see the day when they trundle the Cézannes into the basement.' He raised his glass. 'To the death of all bad art!'

'Cheers', said Henry, drinking. He had begun to revise his opinion of Artie. The night before, he had dismissed him as a Yankee culture-bum of the worst type, compensating for his own inadequacies and fear of ordinary life by clinging to the protracted adolescence of the Left Bank student-tramp. Now, behind the nervous beard, the grating Texan drawl—with its Greenwich Village overlay—and the cynical child's eyes, he detected an unconventional intelligence at work. Artie was his first Paris contact who had brought him any intellectual pleasure. 'Why don't we dine together?' he asked.

'It's a date', said Artie. 'But allow me to select the restaurant. Uncle Sam's monthly culture cheque does not arrive till Monday, and the gold in my Fort Knox is nearing exhaustion. No—don't offer to invite me. I accept money only from women. I know a place near here where you eat well for 400 francs.'

They dined in a small Greek restaurant in the Rue Grégoire de Tours, queueing for places at bare wooden tables. Artie selected the menu—*shish-kebab* with rice dumplings, and gritty red wine poured from earthenware jugs. They drank about a litre each, while Artie discoursed on Left Bank life.

'Don't come to any quick conclusions about it', he said. 'There's truth and fraud here, good and bad, like anywhere else. The only difference is, here the conflict seems bigger and sharper, more important. So much intelligence has been lavished on this place by so many people, from so many countries, and for so many years, that some of it was bound to stick. So everything becomes a little bigger than life-size. Every conversation becomes

51

a drama, every drinking bout a debauch. The small change of politics becomes the future of the human race. Every shop is a microcosm of capitalism, every worker the hero of *Das Kapital*. An artist or a writer is an arbiter of destiny, a walk in the streets is a profound experience. Sex becomes love—or sin. Money becomes happiness— or incarnate evil. The street-cars are portentous, the hotels are universities, the waiters are professors of empirical philosophy—and crooks, too. The result is, life becomes exhausting. Living here is like fighting a war: you emerge dead, crippled or ennobled, but in any event changed.'

'That's exactly it', said Henry, his thoughts ballooning forth from the chaos of wine in his stomach. 'You take me, for instance. What am I supposed to be—a prig or a poet? A cog in some capitalist machine, or a name which will make posterity marvel? *I* don't know. I've come here to find out.'

'So you want to create?' asked Artie. 'Well, I know just the place to take you—the Café Zok. They all want to create there: would-be poets, novelists, movie directors, playwrights, fashion-designers, choreographers, musicians—the lot. And from all over the place, black, white, yellow. We've even got an Aborigine intellectual from Australia. Individually, they're pretty nasty. Collectively, they're horrific. If you can survive *them*— you've got genius, boy.'

'Lead on', said Henry, 'I can't wait to see this Café Zok.'

It lay at the end of a narrow street north of the Boulevard, on the ground floor of a sleazy hotel, much patronized by dubious foreigners. The early nineteenth-century framework of the café—frosted windows, massive, wrought-iron blinds, worked by ponderous machinery, and hard red-plush seats—still survived, but the old copper bar, with its cut-glass mirrors and gas-brackets, had been wrenched out and replaced by a chromatic monstrosity in flesh-coloured Canadian pine and stainless steel. Formica-covered tables jostled against the old banquettes; an Espresso machine throbbed and hissed; and just inside the door there was a clutch of pin-table machines and a juke box of immense size and power. The Café, in fact, was a microcosm of contemporary France —a haphazard mixture of the comfortably old and the brassily modern.

Madame Gobat, the allegedly ex-Collaborationist proprietress, presided over the coffee-machine, sitting on a high stool from which she could observe the activities of her daughter-in-law, a sullen and peaky blonde, who acted as *caissière*. Madame had clearly possessed some claim to beauty at one time, and she still used a great deal of paint, went to an expensive hairdresser who frizzed up her thinning and tinted black curls, and covered her fat fingers with an astonishing variety of diamond and ruby rings. But nothing could halt the inexorable encroachment of her sallow flesh, which swelled out her expensive black satin dresses, plumped her black nylon-clad legs, stuffed into the tightest red ballet shoes, and, inflating her rouged cheeks, pressed down upon her sharp, greedy eyes.

Madame Gobat's eyes watched not only her daughter-in-law: they slid occasionally to her husband, a small, bedraggled man in his sixties, who wore a high winged collar and came into the café every evening to play cards with neighbouring tradesmen; they hovered constantly over Serge, the head waiter, who was saving to buy his own café, and who was therefore potentially dishonest, and over his two broken-down colleagues, who were grossly underpaid and therefore potentially dishonest also. Madame's eyes brooded, too, over the customers: there was a fond glance for a group of Radical Socialist senators, of impeccable conservatism, who had voted the *pleins pouvoirs* to Marshal Pétain, and who dropped in when the bar in the Conseil de la République shut for the evening; and there were flashes of distrustful hostility for the motley collection of creative expatriates who formed the majority of her clients.

These could be divided into three main groups, in descending order of solvency. There were the British and American newspaper correspondents, the professional journalists from the *Herald Tribune* Paris edition, and the English services of the French press agencies and radio. They had regular incomes, drank *fine à l'eau*, and even possessed wives instead of mistresses. But to Madame Gobat's chagrin, they formed the smallest of the three groups; for many of them, the Zok was only a second-choice café, coming after the Deux Magots or the Brasserie Lipp. The largest group were the American 'students'—studying at the Ecole des Beaux Arts or the Sorbonne, at the expense of the U.S. government or one of those bountiful millionaire institutions which seem to exist mainly to prolong the adolescence of the second-grade intellectual into early middle age. The students had regular incomes, too, but they were liable to be spent early in the month; moreover, they tended to drink beer. The third group were of mixed nationalities—English, American, Dutch, German, Scandinavian, Chinese, African, even an occasional Vietnamese or Brazilian. They had virtually no money at all, drank the cheapest red wine, were more drunken, argumentative and pro-miscuous than the rest, but produced the occasional poem, picture, or even book. They were anathema to Madame Gobat, who would have liked to drive them down the road to the Café des Nations, a distinctly inferior establishment, whose owner did not object to an occasional brawl or even a police-raid. But she was reluctantly aware that, if she did so, her other foreign clients might leave also; and though a passion-ate xenophobe, she always placed business before politics.

So much Henry gathered from Artie on the way, and he found the café much as he imagined it: a haze of smoke, tables jumbled with glasses and saucers, dirty-looking girls in men's sweaters and tight trousers, savage or merely sullen young men, with the light of the Absolute in their eyes, their minds restlessly turning over the pages of unwritten manuscripts. There were one or two monumental figures of established authors, each with a circle of satellites: a Negro novelist, an Englishwoman who concocted delicious travel-books, with her French girl-friend, a young Californian whose first play had been performed on Broadway. And there were the myriad editors of the Left Bank quarterlies, many of whom used the Zok as an office, in which they drew up layouts and corrected proofs.

Henry and Artie found a table with difficulty, and ordered beer. Henry noticed that Madame Gobat eyed him with a more appreciative glance than she accorded Artie, who had clearly been irrevocably placed in the third category. The thick, sweaty air and arguments welled up around them.

'. . . if *Angles* won't publish it, I can always go to *Zero*.

They're just about ready for another critical survey of Bertolt Brecht.'

'I hear *Angles* paid Arthur 2,000 francs for his poem about the *pissoirs*.'

'Bloody nepotism. Now I know who Arthur's sleeping with.'

'. . . We must get away from *narrative*.'

'And punctuation.'

'And *mood* prose. How I hate mood prose.'

'Like Samuel Beckett, of course. The No-image.'

'The Un-thing. The Sub-character.'

'The Creative Void.'

'Like Skoplje.'

'And Brakst.'

'Like Christopher Logue . . .'

'. . . anti-imperialism. That's the only thing that matters in contemporary Asia. Take Kassem. A conservative of the old type, you might say, but he loathes your Britisher's guts . . .'

'. . . oil politics. Whitehall has to dance when Standard of New Jersey calls the tune. Take Abadan. . .'

'. . . take Bandaraniaike . . .'

'. . . take Kuwait . . .'

'. . . Nasser said to me . . .'

'. . . I told General Ayub . . .'

'. . . Six miserable paras, down column under a one-line head. It makes you weep blood. And the rumour about Pinay was exclusive.'

'. . . So he says, nobody's indispensable to this newspaper. Check, I says, and no newspaper's indispensable to Robert J. Hopgood, either.'

'*Deux Baby-whisky*, Serge!'

'*Une bière et trois vins rouges*, Serge!'

'. . . What d'ya mean, no more credit? Tell that fat bitch of a *patronne* . . .'

'*Serge!*'

Henry talked to an architect from Dallas about the new Unesco building, on which he held strong opinions, and to a Kenyan Freedom-Fighter about apartheid. He was enjoying himself, so much so that he greeted without displeasure the arrival of Edgar the Poet, who joined their table.

'Greetings, bourgeois', he said to Henry. 'I see it hasn't taken you long to reach this point-of-no-return. Thanks, since you don't suggest it, I will have a drink. Serge, bring me a glass of Beaujolais on this monsieur.' He turned back to Henry. 'I have news for you. You have fairly smitten the curvaceous Dora.'

'What do you mean?' asked Henry, blushing. He had a distinct and embarrassed recollection of the previous night. Had Dora, the unpredictable bitch, gone all over Paris telling people about it?

'Not literally, of course', said Edgar, 'though that, too, might well endear you to her. No, she has evidently succumbed to your charm. At this moment she is roaming the streets looking for you. She has already called, unsuccessfully, on your hotel. Ah, but here she is!'

Dora entered in a swirl of silken skirts. A light fur coat —no doubt a relic of the Rock 'n' Roll period—was flung loosely across her shoulders, her hair was windswept, and her bosom, sharply sculptured under a tight, lime-green shirt, rose and fell energetically. She had evidently been running.

'Henry, darling', she said. 'Thank God I've found you.' Henry rose nervously to his feet. 'Won't you sit down?' he asked.

'Can't, angel. I must simply drag you away this instant. Something frightfully important's happened, which I can't possibly explain here.'

Had she made such a request earlier in the day, it is very likely, or at least possible, that Henry would have refused. Though not a man of strong character, at any rate where women were concerned, he had been very annoyed by the previous night's incident—annoyed not only with Dora, but even more with himself—and anxious to erase this foolish chapter from his mind. But he was now flushed with wine, and his mind was once more crowded with romantic success-fantasies. Moreover Dora was looking even more vulgarly tempting than the night before, and her odd behaviour added to her attractions.

'Will you excuse me?' he said to Artie, fatuously.

'Spare me the Old Etonian line, boy. I never stand between a man and his woman.'

'We can do without the blushes, too', said Edgar. 'They spring from a disturbed class conscience. In a classless society, the sexual act is of no more moral significance than hammering home a rivet in a shipyard.'

'Shut up', said Dora. 'Come along, Henry.'

He followed her into the street, where she hailed a taxi. 'Forgive me for last night', she said, snuggling up to him. 'I was yearning for love and all that, but simply too tired to stay awake. I'm sorry I got mad at you, but you gave me such a whack—I'll show you the bruise. In the right mood, a playful tap's all right, but darling, you don't know your own strength.'

'I'm most frightfully sorry', said Henry desperately. 'I can't think what came over me. I must have been drunk.'

'Don't apologize, darling'. She kissed him on his

cheek. 'But remember the moral: let sleeping girls lie.'

'What do you want to talk to me about?' asked Henry.

'Later, darling, when we get back to the studio, and I've mixed you a drink.'

When they arrived, Henry declined a cocktail, settling for a brandy and soda. The flat was in spotless order, and Henry sat down on a flame-coloured studio couch, which the night before had been a dishevelled and crumb-spattered bed. She fixed the drinks and curled up beside him.

'Look', she said, 'I'll put it to you straight. Kiki's in trouble down in Nice.'

'Oh', said Henry, unable to conceal the disappointment in his tone.

'I don't quite know what sort of trouble. A friend of his telephoned me this afternoon, long-distance. He's had a row with his hotel down there, and the police have arrested him. I've got to get the poor darling out.'

'But how can I help?' asked Henry grudgingly.

'This way. I've booked a seat for myself on the morning plane to Nice tomorrow. It leaves at eight or some bloody awful hour. I know I can fix things if I get down there. I've quite a way with gendarmes and their sort. There's nothing seriously wrong. But I may need some money. That's where you come in.'

'Money? But I thought you had plenty.'

'Not so much at this time of the month. My alimony or what-have-you doesn't come until next week. Besides, I may need quite a bit. I've already hocked a gold wrist-watch, but the miserable French state hock-shops don't give you much. How much can you lend me?'

Among Henry's nicer characteristics was that he never lied about money, or indeed thought much about it either. 'I've got £100 or so in traveller's cheques', he said.

'Good. Give me £80.'

'Eighty!' said Henry. 'But this is supposed to last me three months.'

'Don't worry', said Dora impatiently—she was evidently not used to arguing with men about money. 'You'll get it all back next week, cross my heart. All you need to do is to countersign them, and I'll be able to cash them down there.'

'All right', said Henry reluctantly, taking the cheques from his pocket. He did not think Dora was dishonest, but her careless attitude to money gave him an uneasy feeling that he might never see it again. On the other hand, he had never before been asked for a loan by a woman, and knew that he could not very well refuse such a direct request without implying that he distrusted her. So he laboriously wrote out his signature on the cheques.

'Oh, yes', said Dora. 'And I'll need your passport, too, in case the bank asks for it.'

'No', said Henry firmly, his Englishman-Abroad's most basic instinct outraged by the thought of being passportless among foreigners. 'Money, yes. Passport, no.'

'Well, I suppose you're right. I'll have to wangle it somehow. Thanks for the cheques, anyway. I'll be off first thing tomorrow, and with any luck I'll be back by Monday. And now for another little drinkie.'

They had another little drinkie, and then another. Dora leaned heavily against Henry's shoulder, and as they fell backwards on the studio couch, she drew his mouth towards her moist, parted lips. She seemed worried about Kiki and anxious to be comforted. Henry himself was in a quandary: passionately as he wanted to make love to Dora, he was uneasy lest he should appear to be extracting a *quid pro quo* for his loan. Might not this be Dora's attitude, too? Was she merely rewarding him, passively and dutifully, for allowing her to come to the rescue of her lover? He decided this was not so. Dora was sufficiently direct and demanding to expect him to lend her money without offering anything in return. She was inviting him to sleep with her because she wanted to. He was beginning to realize that it was entirely in character for her to try to allay her anxieties about one man by taking refuge in the arms of another.

'Muss me up a little, darling', she said in an American accent.

Henry clumsily undid the buttons of her blouse and fiddled hopelessly with the fastening on her brassiere. In the end she had to help him.

'Sweet Henry', she whispered, nuzzling his ear. 'You're so nice and inexperienced and terribly, terribly middle-class. I could love you'. She slid a hand into his shirt and felt his heart-beats. 'And so passionate, too. Darling, take me to bed now, please.'

They made love in the large pink bed in Dora's room, Henry in his anxiety doing less than justice to himself. Dora, too, though skilful, experienced and kind, seemed preoccupied. Henry realized there was a third person present: the unfortunate Kiki, damn him. Afterwards, Dora silently rested her head on his shoulder, and he felt her tears on his skin. 'Please don't worry', he said. 'It's all right', said Dora, her voice trembling. 'I don't worry, really. It's just that—why am I such a slut? Why do I go for men like Fan Treffle and Kiki. Why can't I fall for somebody like you, and just be normal? It doesn't make sense.'

She murmured to herself for a time, then dropped into a heavy sleep, her warm breath falling evenly on Henry's bare chest. Henry lay stiff and agonized, terrified to wake her. He had never spent a night with a woman before, and had no idea how one slept in a bed with another person. Each time he moved his shoulder, she stirred uneasily, and it was almost dawn before, exhausted, he slept. When he awoke, two or three hours later, she was gone.

Henry dressed hurriedly, uncomfortably aware that he was alone in a woman's flat. The studio was desolate and deserted. His mouth felt dry from lack of sleep, his money was gone, and so was Dora. Pinned to the door was a note, scrawled, characteristically, in lipstick. It read: 'Back on Monday, darling', and it was signed with three crosses.

Henry trudged back to his hotel, to shave and change. Madame was already presiding behind the desk, and there was a hint of coy appraisal in her voice as she asked him: 'Monsieur passed a pleasant evening, I trust?'

For once, Henry—normally scrupulously polite—did not deign to reply. But later, in his room, as he lathered his face and brushed his teeth strenuously with Colgates, his black mood disappeared. When all was said and done, he told himself, he had spent his first night with a woman.

# III

HENRY passed the next few days in relative tranquillity. The weather changed: soft spring rain fell on the boulevard, glistening the capes of the watchful policemen at the street-corners and washing away the chalk slogans on the walls. But for the moment there was no more trouble. M. Gaillard's government survived its vote of confidence by tabling a new, and entirely formal, motion on Algeria and by increasing the fixed price supports for the beetroot growers and some categories of wine farmers. The dollar fell from 425 to 410 francs. The papers were full of a sensational new Brigitte Bardot film on in the Champs Elysées, and a gruesome multi-murder case in Bayonne.

Henry attended lectures assiduously, on Ronsard, on the court memoirs of Saint-Simon, on the origins of the Paris *couture* industry, illustrated by models lent by the Maison Dior, and on Pascal's *Pensées*. He visited the Cabinet des Médailles in the Bibliothèque Nationale and an exhibition devoted to the relics and manuscripts of Saint-Beuve. He went on a conducted tour of the Hotel Lambert in the Ile-St-Louis and a trip round the Paris sewers. He read about three hundred pages of Proust and two chapters of Professor Brogan. He wrote a six-page letter to his mother and made several lengthy entries in a Lett's diary he had bought especially to record his Paris experiences. He also began to draft the plot of a novel about the adventures of a young man in Paris; but this did not go very well. He spent very little money and drank only a quarter-carafe of wine a day. He accumulated culture and virtue simultaneously.

His social life also made progress. On Friday evening, Henry made acquaintance with M. Hurlot, the Communist deputy. who lived in the next room. Henry was about to go to bed when there was a tap on his door, and there was M. Hurlot, a short, stooping gentleman of about sixty, dressed in shiny black trousers, a hand-knitted cardigan, black tie and black alpaca jacket. He invited Henry to have some coffee, cooked, quite illegally but with the connivance of Madame, on a spirit stove in his room.

The room was a little larger than Henry's but appeared far smaller, for it was cluttered with furniture and bric-à-brac. M. Hurlot explained that he had lived there for fifteen years, ever since his wife died, and that the room held all his worldly possessions. There was a huge Second Empire armchair, with ear-flaps, a heavy Louis Seize looking-glass framed in malachite, and a Chinoiserie cupboard which M. Hurlot said had once belonged to Jean Jaurès. On the wall were framed portraits of Dimitrov, Maurice Thorez (signed '*A mon cher camarade Hurlot*'), and Mao Tse-tung; there was also a faded coloured print of Marshal Foch, under whom M. Hurlot had served in Champagne in 1918. The old gentleman had other treasures: a manuscript letter signed by Dreyfus, an inkstand which had been used by Clemenceau, and the order for his own arrest, in 1944, signed by Pétain.

While M. Hurlot made the coffee, in a battered old Algerian copper jug, he told Henry all about himself. He was a watch-maker from the Ardèche, who had become a union official. During the last war he had joined a Communist resistance group—he had been a member of the C.P., he told Henry proudly, ever since the Schism of Tours in 1921—and had helped to liberate Paris. At the time of the Constituent Assembly in 1944, the Communists had adopted him as a candidate for a very conservative rural *département* in the Massif Central, which always voted Communist. He had remained a deputy ever since. He attended regularly, but had never been asked to speak by the party leaders; in fact he did not like public speaking, although he was always delighted to join in the *bruits a l'extrème gauche* and the *claquement des pupîtres* which took place in the Assembly whenever a right-wing deputy made a particularly offensive remark. He showed Henry his technique for banging the lid of his desk to create the maximum possible noise. He had also, he said, on one occasion hurled a copy of the *Cahiers de Marxisme* at the head of an M.R.P. minister; but he rather regretted it now—it was un-parliamentary.

Henry, sitting in the huge armchair, drank the hot, bitter coffee, while M. Hurlot mumbled on, fiddling with press-cuttings and letters in his files. He seemed a lonely old soul, with no friends outside formal acquaintances in the party, and only too anxious to talk to a stranger. 'But you understand', he said, 'I do not talk to people outside the hotel. Somebody might see me, and the party might not understand.' His attitude to the party, in fact, was exactly the same as a Victorian child towards its father: a blend of fear and respect, tinged occasionally with flashes of affection. His eyesight was fading: he could no longer make or repair watches, so his job in the Assembly was very important to him. 'It is a good job, you know, because although the hours are sometimes

65

very long, and attendance for us is strict, specially now we have to vote in person on the confidence motions, we have long vacations and the pay is very good.' His salary was about £2,500 a year, in theory; but two-thirds of this was paid direct into the party's bank. The rest he was allowed to keep. Most of this he sent to his invalid brother in Bordeaux, who had been tortured by the Vichy *milice*; he himself lived quite happily on 30,000 francs a month, and drank a glass of *fine* every evening after dinner. He had also, he confided to Henry as a great secret, subscribed to the Pinay Loan, which although condemned by the party, was rigged to the price of gold and therefore was a good investment for a poor Frenchman such as himself. He had other shares, too, which he showed Henry—tattered pieces of franked paper, dating back to the early Thirties some of them, and now mostly worthless: ten of them came from Stavisky's famous pawnshop, which had produced the big scandal in 1934. M. Hurlot had taken part in the great riot on 6 February, not because he agreed with the Fascists, but because he wanted his money back. 'You see', he told Henry soberly, 'only the party will look after the money of poor folks like myself. When we come to power, I have been promised a big job in the Ministry of Commerce, as a *chef de service* with an office to myself and a secretary with pink fingernails and a tight skirt. But perhaps', he added sadly, 'I shall be too old by then.'

'But is there a crisis coming?' asked Henry.

'Yes. But perhaps not. My brother-in-law, who has a farm in the Jura, got good prices for his heifers last month. Many of the workers are living well. It is like the Twenties, before the big crash. But the Fascists are strong too, again. It may be necessary to recall De Gaulle. He is a good man. I wept tears when he shook my hand in July 1944.'

'But I thought your party was opposed to De Gaulle', said Henry sharply.

'Yes. But perhaps not. He is a big fellow, a *ténor*, and sometimes difficult to get on with. I do not say he is without faults, and of course he is a Catholic, with two Jesuits in each pocket. But France is an old country. It is not right that she should be pushed around so much. Maybe we should have De Gaulle again, to put the foreigners in their place.' For the first time a glint of animation came into his eyes. 'Why did you British have to sell arms to our enemies in Tunisia?'

'Now look here', said Henry, 'You're a Communist and your party is opposed to the Algerian war. You should be in favour of the rebels getting arms.'

The glint of animation died. 'We are opposed to all wars and all arms.' M. Hurlot sighed deeply. 'I do not claim to understand everything about politics, young man. You must remember I have no great education, though I read my Pascal every day. I understand watches and farming—my father was a cattle-dealer. And now let me show you my wedding photographs.'

It was nearly one o'clock before Henry got away, after accepting a copy of M. Hurlot's last election address. He had always regarded hotels as private, impersonal places, where solitary individuals led separate lives. But this was not so of the Paris-Palace, and during the next week he got to know most of its permanent residents. Opposite him was Madame Salbert, a buxom blonde in her early forties, who sang comic songs at a *bal musette* in the XV arrondissement; at least, this is what she told Henry, but she showed no enthusiasm

67

when he enquired the address of the *bal* and offered to
go and hear her one evening. According to the chambermaid, Odette—who turned out to be fat, dirty and in no
danger of having her *pudeur* outraged by Henry or
indeed anyone else—she was paid a weekly pension by
a commercial traveller from Orleans, who visited her on
Mondays, Wednesdays and Fridays. Madame Salbert
also invited Henry to evening coffee—it was her night
off, she explained—and he accepted only with some
reluctance, especially after he saw she was wearing a
faded pink dressing-gown, trimmed with fawn fur, which
revealed quantities of her well-developed bosom. But
she was plainly not interested in seducing him: she
merely wanted to grumble about the hotel to a sym-
pathetic audience. Her coffee-pot was a fine piece of old
blue Sèvres, decorated in the Chinese Lowestoft style,
with a gilt dragon for a handle; and her black-and-gold
coffee cups had each an embossed pink rose at the
bottom.

'You will have noticed, Monsieur', she began, 'that
Odette is a slut. Her person is filthy, so that I cannot bear
the smell of her when she comes into my room in the
morning. Her dusting is outrageous—I recently discovered a cobweb at the back of my wardrobe. On the
days she cleans the wash-basin she does not clean the
*bidet*, and vice versa. Exhortation and abuse is useless.
Complaint to Madame Marcourt equally so. Despite
the fact that she is aware I was born in a Château, and
that my profession demands a minimum of comfort and
attention, she remains indifferent to my complaints, and
has even had the insolence to suggest that I move elsewhere. No doubt you have formed a similarly unfavour-
able impression of our proprietress?'

'Well', said Henry cautiously, 'she is clearly a business-woman.'

'Exactly, Monsieur. A hard-faced franc-grubber from Toulouse. Her mother, who was, needless to say, unmarried, owned a workman's bar in the worst quarter of the city. I have it on the best authority that Madame Marcourt began her career as a five-franc *poule*. How she rose to her present elevated position'—here Madame Salbert tittered theatrically, and drew her dressing-gown together—'it is not for me to speculate upon. I notice that her husband is conveniently dead. You are aware, of course, that she is conducting a sordid, indeed public, affair with a young government chauffeur? No? But then young Englishmen are inclined to be unobservant about these things. But sordid is the word. I have seen this man strutting arrogantly out of her room, naked to the waist, wearing only his breeches and leggings. But this, note well, does not prevent her from complaining on the rare occasions when *I* entertain a visitor—and adding an extra charge to my bill! She has even maliciously drawn my attention to the *règlement* which forbids one to make coffee in one's room, although I know that that disgusting Communist across the corridor does exactly the same with impunity. And others, too. That disagreeable Indian journalist on the second floor, for example. To judge by the smells he even cooks curry in his room. This hotel has deteriorated very much since I first came here six years ago. The clientele—and naturally I except you, Monsieur, from this, for you are clearly a gentleman of good family—has become less select. More coffee?'

'No thank you', said Henry. The coffee was thin, and flavoured with lavender.

'A little Crème de Menthe, perhaps?'

'Please no,' said Henry. 'I must go to bed soon—I have a lot of studying, you know.'

'Ah, yes—you have come here to learn about French culture. A noble vocation, Monsieur. France has so much to offer and teach the world. But you must improve your accent: it is disagreeable to French ears to hear their beautiful language misused. As a nation, you understand, we are misused in every way these days. But a change is coming—as a woman I can feel it. La France will reassert herself. The corrupt politicians, the Jews and the Communists will be thrown out. We shall soon have a strong man to guide our destiny again—you shall see. . . But as I was saying, you must improve your accent. Do you know what you should do?'

'No' said Henry, replacing his coffee-cup and standing up.

'You must meet a young Parisienne for conversation. That is the way to learn. Since you are a respectable and studious young man, I think perhaps I can arrange it. I have a niece in Paris, a young, charming, educated girl of good family, who I think I could persuade to help you. You could meet her several times a week, perhaps. She would be a companion to you, for you are no doubt a little lonely in this strange city. I will speak to her to-morrow.'

'Please don't', said Henry anxiously. 'That is—I must think about it, you know. You're very kind to be so thoughtful.' He edged towards the door.

Madame Salbert laughed. 'I know you are thinking she is very plain, with spectacles and protuding teeth. You are wrong monsieur, she is *mignonne*—a charmer— and not averse to the delicate attentions of young men,

I can assure you. You will enjoy her company. . . .' She followed him across the room, her dressing-gown swaying open precariously.

'I'm sorry', said Henry, with a trace of desperation. 'But you know I have no money to pay for lessons.'

'Money', said Madame Salbert sharply. 'That is not a very nice thing to mention to a lady. But I see what you mean. Lessons have to be—paid for. A girl does not like a young man without a *sou* in his pocket. A pity. But nevertheless, it has been pleasant to make your acquaintance. *Bon soir, monsieur!*'

'Good night', said Henry.

There were other odd, if less menacing, residents in the hotel—an elderly conjurer, who specialized in children's parties, and his wife, who had once worked in a circus. They lived above Henry, and occasionally awoke him by violent crashes in the night. Was he practising conjuring tricks, or was she reviving memories of the Big Top? There was Monsieur Van Dien, who had once been a government stooge for the French in Indo-China, and who had been forced to leave when the crash came. Unlike most of his colleagues, he had been either too honest or too stupid to make a fortune out of black market currency deals, and was now living in poverty, travelling every day by bus to the Bibliothèque Nationale, where he was writing a definitive account of the *affaire des piastres*. From time to time he stopped Henry on the stairs to tell him a freshly discovered item of outrageous scandal connected with some prominent government personality. Then there was a middle-aged compatriot, Mr. Birkett, a tall, raw-boned Scot who worked in one of the English banks. Birkett gave Henry a cheerful greeting each time they met. His ruddy, honest face topped with a short thatch of greying hair was solidly reassuring among this sea of insane foreigners; but he never offered to talk and had a reputation for extreme reticence in the hotel. It was generally supposed he was a member of the British Secret Service.

Henry also began to make friends at the Sorbonne. Through Shirley-Anne, another resident at his hotel, he met a succession of American girl students, each almost indistinguishable from the rest, with their boys' shorts, knee-socks, button-shoes and check shirts. They carried satchels of books and spent a great deal of time sucking Coca-Cola through straws at the Dupont brasserie in the Boulevard St. Michel. Most of them lived in the American hostel in the Cité Universitaire and were indubitably virgins. Together with a group of crew-cut American boys, who had similarly refused to go native, they formed what was clearly the slow set among the U.S. student colony. The fast set, which included half-a-dozen very pretty girls, who wore skirts instead of trousers, revolved around two Harvard seniors, who possessed a Jaguar and an Alfa-Romeo respectively. They were on visiting terms with the American Embassy and were reputed to hold marijuana parties in the Jaguar's Montparnasse apartment.

Henry found neither of these circles particularly attractive; he was beginning to form that vague distaste for Americans which is one of the by-products of residence in Paris. Towards the end of his second week, he found himself becoming just a little bored and even lonely. He twice went down to the Café at the bottom of the Rue Bonaparte, but failed to find his two Communist friends. He paid a call on a French family to whom he had been given a letter of introduction, but was told by the servant that

72

they were away. One afternoon, with a certain sense of guilt, he even went to the Café Zok, but found nobody there whom he knew.

He was beginning to miss Dora and her friends. He was also becoming seriously worried about money. Dora had promised to return to Paris the Monday after her departure. He had not expected her to stick to this, but it was now nearly a fortnight later, and he had heard nothing from her. In order to settle his first fortnight's hotel bills, he had been forced to cash his remaining traveller's cheques, and he now had only 10,000 francs in hand. With economy, this would last him another fortnight, but no more.

On Sunday evening—that is, over a fortnight after Dora's departure—Henry totted up his resources and decided to take action. From his hotel he telephoned Dora's apartment, but there was no reply; or rather, there was a peculiar dialling tone. There was obviously something wrong with Dora's telephone; or perhaps it had been cut off. He tried again, half an hour later, with the same result. Finally, at about half past nine, he set out for Dora's house, climbed the dark stairs, and knocked on the door. There was no reply, and he knocked harder. From inside came a faint sound of movement, and Henry struck the door another thunderous blow.

After a minute's fiddling with the latch, the door opened, revealing a girl Henry had never seen before. She was tying a dressing gown over a pair of dark green pyjamas. Her feet were bare. Coils of thick black hair fell over her face, which was puffed with sleep, and she found some difficulty in focusing her eyes, which were half-shut, on Henry.

'Blast you', she said in an American accent. 'You

73

would wake me up just after I've taken a couple of tablets. What do you want?'

'Can I speak to Dora?' asked Henry.

'Who's Dora?' The girl yawned.

'Well, the girl who owns this apartment.'

'*I* own this apartment, mister.'

'Are you sure?' asked Henry fatuously. 'I mean, I thought Dora—Lady Treffle—owned it.'

'You thought wrong.' The girl began to shut the door.

'I say', said Henry, 'please don't go. I'm most awfully sorry to disturb you, but I really don't understand. Dora was living here a fortnight ago, and it's rather important I should see her.'

'This Dora—was she a fat red-haired trambo with an outsize bust?'

'Well, I suppose you might choose to describe her as that.'

'I do choose. She isn't here, and I have no idea of her present whereabouts. And, let me tell you, she should never have been here in the first place. When I went away to the States a couple of months back, I lent this apartment to an English boy. He introduced the Dora doll here, without my permission.'

'Was the man called Kiki?'

'That wasn't the name he gave me, mister. As I was saying, when I got back last week, I found both of them here, so I threw both of them out. Does that satisfy your curiosity?'

'Yes—I mean, no. You can't tell me where they are now?'

'In some bar, I guess. And now, if you'll kindly allow me, I'll shut my door.'

She did so, firmly, and Henry was left on the dark

74

landing. He was now in a mood bordering between rage and panic. Dora had lied to him about the apartment. She had probably also lied about her ability to return his money. She had been back in Paris at least a week without attempting to get in touch with him. And where the hell was she anyway? In some bar with the infamous Kiki, who was now emerging as a thorough scoundrel.

Henry hurried to the Café Zok, narrowly escaping sudden death as he crossed the boulevard. The café was crowded and he scanned the joyful and sullen faces anxiously, but there was no sign of Dora. At one of the tables, however, he saw Edgar, who was playing chess. Henry hurried over.

'Can you tell me where Dora is, please?' he asked.

Edgar looked up, then looked down again at the board, paused for a full thirty seconds, and moved one of his knights.

'Check', he said, and turned to look up at Henry again. 'What did you say?'

'Do you know where Dora is?' said Henry, unable to keep a note of irritation out of his voice.

'My dear man', said Edgar, grinning maliciously, 'I am not a public information service. Moreover, I should have thought that you would be in closer touch with Dora's movements than myself. But I forget—the lover from the South has returned. Hence your distress. Let me look at you: there is nothing so poignant as a bourgeois rudely parted from his woman.'

'To hell with that', said Henry angrily. 'I'm not interested in Dora as a woman. I merely happen to have lent her a large sum of money.'

'Ho Ho!' said Edgar, crowing with glee. 'Even more

poignant is the spectacle of a bourgeois rudely parted from his money.'

He dodged to one side as Henry stretched out an exasperated hand to clutch at the lapels of his leather jacket. 'Now then, no violence. Serge wouldn't like it, nor would Madame Gobat. I am not Colonel Nasser, nor are you Sir Anthony Eden. I'm afraid you've made a bad investment: Dora is gilt-edged in looks, in charm also, but not in substance. Seriously, my dear man, I doubt if you will see your money again. At the risk of sounding curious, how much was it?'

'Eighty pounds.'

Edgar whistled. 'Yes—I see your point. What are you going to do now—become a prole like the rest of us and starve? Let me welcome you to our band.'

'No, I'm going to find her. Are you sure you don't know where she'll be?'

'Let me think. I hear that she and her boy-friend are in some hotel somewhere, but I don't know which one. Anyway, they're sure to be out at this time of evening. You might try the Sélect, in Montparnasse, or even the Dôme. They might be in Lipp, or the Deux Magots, or the Flore. Or the Montana or the Village—they're just off the Boulevard St. Germain. If they're in none of these, try the little bars in the Rue Grégoire de Tours. I forget all their names, but just go up the street looking in each.'

'Thanks', said Henry. 'I'm very grateful.'

'Not at all. Let me wish you good hunting. Eighty quid, by jove. That's a blow for the City!'

Henry trudged up to Montparnasse, but drew a blank at all the big cafés. He walked rapidly back along the Rue de Rennes, and looked in at Lipp and the Flore and the Deux Magots. After a great deal of questioning, he found the Montana and the Village, too, but no sign of Dora. It was now after eleven, and Henry was beginning to despair of finding her that evening. He felt tired, cold and no longer even angry.

He walked slowly back to his hotel along the boulevard. There was a café on the left, with a raised *terrasse*, which called itself the Rhumerie de Guadeloupe. Outside, a sign advertised: 'Rhum au Lait Chaud—100 francs'. Rum and hot milk: that at least would make him sleep! Henry decided to invest some of his remaining capital, and went inside. And there, of course, was Dora.

She was sitting at a corner table, surrounded by three men. A light blue scarf was tied round her neck, and a blue-and-gold butterfly, of considerable vulgarity, glittered in her hair; the fur coat and the tight shirt were the same as on the night she had borrowed Henry's money. Flushed and laughing, she looked like an Edwardian chorus girl out for supper with a cohort of young cavalry officers. Indeed, two of the men with her, who flanked her on both sides and who were strangers to Henry, seemed to fit the scene: both wore blazers and striped ties, and had the slightly offensive and decaying good looks of young members of the English upper-middle class. The third man, who wore a sweater and a silk square, had his back to Henry. All had evidently been there some time: the table was loaded with glasses and saucers, and the ash-tray was piled high with smouldering cigarettes.

Henry walked over slowly, his hands in his pockets. 'Good evening, Dora', he said, keeping his voice on what he hoped was a calm and even tone.

She looked up, and there was, he noted grimly, not

77

the slightest trace of embarrassment on her face. *'Darling!'* she said in her loud, warm voice. 'How marvellous to see you. Take a pew.'

'Join the happy throng, old boy', said one of the cavalry officers. The blazer, on closer inspection, looked a little dubious; the tie was unknown to Henry; and the accent was distinctly Soho drinking-club.

'Boys', said Dora, 'this is Henry, one of my dearest friends. Henry, this is Bertie and Roger'—she gestured towards the two men in blazers—'and this is Kiki'.

For the first time Kiki looked round, and Henry instantly recognized the arched black eyebrows, the lazy, heavy-lidded eyes, the broad handsome nose and the square—slightly too square—chin of Michael Crick. The face had grown a little fuller, and there was a dark, purplish colour in the shaded hollows under his eyes. But there was no mistaking the coldly mocking grin and the air of contemptuous superiority of his tormentor at school and college. Crick recognized him, too.

'Henry Arnold', he said. 'Artful Arnold, the lady-killer from Wimbledon Common! My dear old chum from Cranpole. This calls for a celebration. Who would have thought we would meet again in the City of Light. *Garçon!*'

'Do you know each other?' asked Dora. 'Well, really.'

'Of course we do, eh Henry? Since we were so high. Heaved together in the scrum, swotted together in the Remove, queued together outside the Head's study. Many's the scrape we've been in together in those far-off gilded days at Cranpole. Where's that bloody waiter? Hoy, Peasant! *Venez vite!*'

'How nice', said Dora sentimentally.

'We were never in the same class', said Henry coldly.

78

'And I can't say we knew each other very well, either. As a matter of fact, I'm surprised to see you here, Crick. I'd heard you were in prison in Singapore.'

Crick's smile vanished, if only for an instant. 'Oh, you'd heard that, had you? Well, you'd heard wrong, old boy. Rumours get around, you know—doesn't do to believe all of them.'

'Really? I seem to remember this was a pretty well-substantiated rumour. Newspaper cuttings and all that.'

This time the smile disappeared completely. Crick turned to Dora. 'Dora, my sweet', he said. 'I don't think I like your friend. He seems one of the nosy variety. I think we'd perhaps better ask your friend to go away, hadn't we?'

'My friend!' said Dora. 'I like that. I thought you said he was your friend.' For the first time she looked a little uneasy. One of the blazer-men said, 'Why don't we all have a drink?'

'Did you hear?' said Crick, turning round to Henry. 'We don't like you here. Why don't you play space-ships and blast off?'

He had evidently had a number of drinks: there was an ugly, aggressive look in his bloodshot eyes. But Henry was determined to stand his ground. He had disliked and feared Crick for a good many years, but now the fear was overlaid with anger. That Dora had deceived him was now beside the point: he saw Crick as the sole cause of his current predicament. Crick had been living with Dora in the American girl's flat—hence the volume of Wordsworth's poems stolen from the Cranpole library. He had gone down to Nice, probably in pursuit of some girl, and had got into a sordid scrape from which Dora had rescued him with *his* money. The thought that his

79

£80—now probably irredeemable—had been used to save the odious Crick from punishment filled Henry with a fury which he was finding increasingly difficult to control.

'There's no question of my going', he said. 'I have private business with Dora.'

'Have you?' said Crick loudly. 'Let's get one thing clear, old son. Dora's private business is my private business, understand? So if you've got anything to say, out with it.'

'Hear, hear!' said one of the blazer-men, suddenly.

Crick turned on him. 'And that goes for you too, smart Alec. You can take your great lecherous paw off Lady Treffle's knee.'

'I say!' said the young man.

'Oh, shut up, Kiki', said Dora. 'What is it you want, Henry?'

Henry now saw that he had no alternative but to ask Dora for his money in public. Normally, he would have been outraged by the very notion of such a scene, but he was too far gone in anger and misery to care.

'When are you going to return me the money I lent you?' he asked. 'I'm afraid I need it now, and it's already a fortnight overdue.'

'Money?' said Dora. 'What money? Oh—yes, I remember: you did give me some. I didn't quite realize it was a loan, however.'

'Of course it was a loan', said Henry angrily. 'You promised to pay it back as soon as your alimony came through.'

'Did I? Well yes, darling, but it hasn't, you know. That awful ex-husband of mine has been making difficulties. All sorts of legal complications I don't understand. But my lawyers say they can put things right, perhaps.'

'In short, you borrowed my money under false pretences. You're little better than a thief.'

'Listen here', shouted Crick angrily, half rising out of his chair. 'How dare you call Dora a thief! Get out of here, you pimple-faced little bastard, before I throw you out!'

'For God's sake, Kiki, calm down', said Dora. 'Everyone in the place is looking at us.'

'Then what's all this about money?' asked Crick, leaning across the table.

'It's all your fault, Kiki. If only you'd listen I'll explain. When you had that row down in Nice, I had to get hold of some cash somehow, and Henry kindly produced it . If it hadn't been for Henry you'd still be in that gaol.'

Crick sat back in his chair, the sullen anger in his face slowly changing to bewilderment and then to uproarious mirth. His hands gripped the arms of his chair and he threw back his head in a convulsion of savage laughter.

'You mean to say', he said breathlessly, pointing at Henry, 'that this poor tyke here provided the wherewithal? That I owe my release from the cooler to the generosity and filthy lucre of my old pal Artful Arnold? That's rich! That really does beat everything. Eighty bloody quid! My dear Doctor Arnold, I am your eternal, grateful and humble servitor. I shall daily remember you in my prayers. Allah shall reward you!' He placed the tips of his fingers on his forehead and made a low bow of obeisance in Henry's direction.

'Look out!' screamed Dora. 'He's going to hit you!'

But it was too late. Henry, who had not been in a fight

since his prep-school days, and then only in despairing self-defence, launched an aggressive blow for the first time in his life. He aimed his left fist in a wild swing in the general direction of Crick's head. It struck Crick on the shoulder, rather towards the end of its trajectory, and in normal circumstances would have done no damage. But Crick, in making his bow to Henry, had leaned drunkenly forward in his chair; the blow caught him off balance, and he plunged headlong into the table, clutching out desperately. His left hand caught Henry's sleeve, and Henry, somewhat off balance himself from the force and sweeping momentum of his blow, collapsed on top of Crick's back as he surged forward on to the table. There was a sound of rending wood as the weight of the two bodies wrenched the top of the table from its supports. Glasses and saucers catapulted through the air, drenching the nearby clients in beer and *rhum au lait*. Dora jumped to her feet, screaming. The two young men in blazers anxiously pulled out handkerchiefs to wipe the spatterings of alcohol from their clothes. Two waiters, who had been watching the corner table for some time with growing anxiety, marched purposefully forward.

Henry's first reaction, when he found himself floundering on the floor, with Crick beneath him, was to launch a second blow at the elusive head, this time from short range and with the certainty of hitting his target. But amidst the whirling arms and legs, one of the struts of the table—a complex and lethal affair in Baroque bronze—appeared to leap out of the ground and strike him a glancing blow on his chin. For the second time he missed, and on this occasion his fist rammed down upon the broken stem of a wine glass and blood spurted forth. Before he could aim a third blow at the squirming Crick, strong arms seized him from behind, and he found himself being carried, or rather dragged, to the door by two frantic waiters.

'Let me go!' he shouted. 'I've got to deal with that scoundrel in there.' By way of reply, one of the waiters—a Spaniard with cruel eyes and a luxurious black moustache—struck him a vicious blow in the eye with his elbow. The other pummelled his stomach. Together, they forced him down the wooden steps of the *terrasse* and on to the pavement. Their original intention, no doubt, was simply to get him clear of the interior of the café, before he could do any more damage. But once outside, they both remembered the damage he had already done, and turned on him fiercely.

'You pay now', said the Spaniard. 'Fifty thousand francs.'

'Go to hell!' said Henry. 'And let go of my arms, you brute.'

He twisted fiercely to one side, and in a moment of inspiration, brought one of his knees up sharply. It struck the second waiter heavily on the chin, and all three crashed against the side of the *terrasse* and slid to the pavement in a welter of evergreen foliage. Henry, with the strength of despair, tore himself free and ran blindly up the alleyway to the left of the café.

It was the second time he had fled from justice since his arrival in Paris, but this time there was no pursuit. He heard confused shouting, both from outside the café, where the waiters were bellowing for the police, and from inside where, no doubt, Crick was being dealt with by other menials. Ten seconds later came the shrill blast of a Paris police whistle. As Henry hurried into the Rue de Seine, merely walking fast now, so as not to attract attention, he thought with grim satisfaction that Dora, the two spivs in blazers, and above all Crick, hopelessly trapped, every one of them, inside the café, would have to pay for all the damage, and with any luck might even be charged with some frightful criminal offence (somebody had once told him that to start a fight in France was a very serious matter, and heavily punished). The knowledge that Crick was certainly in the soup again might not entirely compensate for the £80, but it went some considerable way towards numbing the pain of loss which burned in Henry's bosom.

Not all the way, however, by any means. Back in his hotel room, which he had managed to regain without exhibiting his dishevelled condition to Madame Marcourt, who was fortunately off duty, he began to assess the damage. His coat had been torn in three places—including a jagged, diagonal tear down the back—and there was a vast right-angled split across the seat of his flannel trousers. On the left-hand side of his head, just above his eye, was a purple bruise, visibly swelling, and his other eye already bore signs of the waiter's elbow. Small pieces of glass were embedded in both his knees, and blood still oozed from a deep gash on his hand, where it had come in contact with the wine-glass stem.

Henry took off his clothes slowly, noticing as he did so that there were other tender spots on his body. He piled his coat and trousers—clearly ruined beyond repair, and bloody too—into the wastepaper basket; then thought again, retrieved them and locked them into one of his suitcases. He staggered to the recess in the corner, drew back the shower-curtain and turned on the hot tap. Icy water gushed forth, but Henry plunged in nevertheless, twitching and moaning as the water stung his cuts and bruises. Presently the water turned warm, and finally hot; Henry washed his wounds and luxuriated in the relaxing steam and heat. After five minutes, he turned off the tap, seized a towel and limped slowly to the bed. Then he remembered the packet of medical supplies his mother had insisted he should bring with him. He took it out and extracted three pieces of elastic dressing, which he applied to his knees and hand. Then, without even pulling back the bedclothes or turning off the light, he fell devastatingly asleep.

He was awakened by a scream, and caught a confused glimpse of Odette's startled face as she retreated, giggling, behind the door. He realized he was lying, stark naked, on top of his bed, and leapt to his feet, searching blindly for his dressing-gown. As he did so, his aches and pains rushed back at him, and with them the memories of his wild evening. He limped to the washbasin and peered critically into the mirror. All things considered, he had been lucky. The bump on the side of his head had largely subsided, and the angry purple colour had disappeared. His other eye had not, as he expected, turned black; there was merely a smear of pale blue in the corner. His hand did not appear to have bled during the night. He was still stiff and sore, but there was clearly no permanent damage. Henry examined his teeth: all perfect. His glance fell on his watch, which lay on the top of the washbasin. It was nearly ten o'clock. He had slept for eleven hours.

Henry began to shave rapidly. Considering his battering, and the fearful risks he had run the night before, he felt remarkably well and even pleased with himself. To become involved in a desperate tavern fight and escape

85

with merely a few cuts and bruises was no mean achievement. He was getting into the swing of Paris life, beginning to untwist the twin strands of intellect and violence which seemed to constitute it. On the other hand, he recognized, quite dispassionately, that his whole existence in the city was now in jeopardy. The £80 were clearly gone for good. Dora had no means of raising them, he felt sure, and Crick would not allow her to even if she could. How, then, was he to live? His next money was not due to arrive for at least another two months. At the most he could survive another fortnight in Paris. He could not, he decided firmly, write home and ask for more money to be sent immediately. This would mean telling the truth about the £80: for, though Henry avoided giving a correct account of his doings to his parents, he though it inadmissible to tell them a direct lie. And if he told the truth about Dora, not only would his father be furious but he would forfeit all his mother's sympathy also. His mother would probably forgive him for losing money in gambling, or even in straightforward debauchery; but he would never be able to explain to her how he had come to lend a large sum of money to a girl who was in love with another man whom he hated. She would regard this as unspeakably sordid, and indeed, in retrospect, it appeared rather sordid to him, too. No: if he told the truth, it would mean returning to London and the victory of his father, an irrevocable sentence to the City or even to chambers. Somehow or other, he would have to find a means of raising money.

He finished shaving and dressed in a grey flannel suit, which he judged appropriate for a man in search of money in a strange city. He also put on his Trinity tie, which he had not worn since he came down. Then he went downstairs.

Madame Marcourt was waiting for him behind the desk. 'I must remind you, Monsieur Arnold', she said, 'that the *pudeur* of Odette is to be respected. She complains that when she entered your room this morning—'

'I know', said Henry. 'I heard her squeal. But then why didn't she knock?' He gave Madame Marcourt what was intended to be a roguish wink. It was not entirely successful, for Henry had never winked at a woman before, and it was a sign of his present curious exhilaration that he made the effort at all. But it achieved its effect: Madame Marcourt smiled wanly.

'I can overlook it this time, Monsieur', she said. Then the smile vanished. 'But I cannot overlook the fact that you left your electric light burning all night. To forget to wear clothes costs no money; to forget to turn the light off does. You will find an additional charge on your next bill.'

'As you please', said Henry. 'By the way, are there any letters for me?'

'No, Monsieur. But a gentleman called for you half an hour ago. I told him you were not yet up, and he said he would wait for you in the Café des Deux Magots. He said his business was important.'

A chill of fear struck at Henry's composure. Who could it be? The police? But they would have waited at the hotel, or even hammered at his door. An emissary from the Crick camp? Much more likely.

'What sort of a man?' he asked.

'Who can say?' said Madame indifferently. 'Small, with a sharp face. A foreigner.'

'Thanks', said Henry. He left the hotel, pondering. The man sounded like Edgar. He was in league with Dora. If Crick had been arrested, Dora would be anxious to get hold of him, in order to prove to the police that he was the real culprit, who had started the fight. She evidently knew the name of his hotel. But if she did know where he lived, why had she not sent the police to him directly?

He crossed to the far side of the Boulevard St. Germain, and peered at the Café des Deux Magots from behind a newspaper stall. The *terrasse* was deserted. He walked across and looked cautiously through the glass swing doors. The room was almost empty, but on the left hand side, sitting alone in front of a cup of coffee, was Edgar. He felt he could deal with Edgar, unless—and this was highly unlikely—Dora and her allies were concealed elsewhere in the room, waiting to spring out at him. He walked into the café.

'Hello, Edgar', he said, taking the seat opposite him at the table. 'You wanted to have a word with me, I hear.'

'My dear boy!' Edgar studied him intently. 'No serious damage, I see. Merely one slight bruise. Let me congratulate you. Your bourgeois trappings are disappearing one by one. First you lose your money, next you are the undoubted victor in a desperate tap-room brawl. A handy man for the barricades, clearly.'

'Thanks', said Henry drily, 'and now what do you want?'

'No call for suspicion, my good fellow: I'm entirely on your side. Crick is not one of my friends, I can assure you. He is perhaps the only man in this part of the world who has never bought me a drink. Moreover, his tem-

88

porary absence from the scene will do no harm to Dora, either.'

'Temporary absence?'

'Ah—I see you are not fully posted on developments. The telephones have been buzzing this morning, I can tell you. First a desperate summons from Crick, from some *boîte de police*, asking me if I was prepared to bail him out or, alternatively, invoke the British consul. I ask you: do I look like a bailing man? Naturally, I refused, with some relish. As for the consul, I am not in the habit of taking tea with him, and I fear that my intercession would produce the opposite result to that desired by Crick. I was therefore able to give Crick small comfort, though I half promised to write a short ode drawing attention to his wrongs and his unjust incarceration.'

'And what about Dora?' asked Henry.

'Dora was the next to telephone, and from her I received a slightly more coherent account of what took place last night, and of the part you played in it. It seems that after your escape—on which I must again congratulate you for your presence of mind—the frustrated servants of the Rhumerie de Guadeloupe turned with some fury on Crick, and dealt him several hefty blows. Dora's two other male companions did not escape injury either, though Dora herself, bless her, was unmolested. Afterwards, the wretched Crick was handed over to the custody of the police, who had been summoned on your behalf, and carted off to the police station behind the Eglise St. Germain. His protests that you were the cause of the *émeute* proved unavailing, but Dora's tearful entreaties appear to have persuaded the management not to prefer charges provided the damage is made good. The damage, I am delighted to add, is substantial—some

150,000 francs. Until it is paid, Crick remains behind bars. And from what I gathered from Dora, it's likely to be some considerable time. Funds, it seems, are low.'

'Serves them bloody well right', said Henry viciously. 'Dammit, they spent my £80.'

'Exactly. And it was precisely about that which I wanted to see you. It is, I fear, lost for ever, and I was anxious to hear what you intended to do now.'

'What can I do? My next allowance is not due for over two months. Unless I can earn some money, I shall have to go back to London.'

'As I thought. And no doubt resume your bourgeois existence as before. An intolerable prospect, now that you are half-way to conversion. It is essential that you remain in Paris to complete your education. I see you agree. And this, my dear Henry—if I may so call you—is where I come in.'

'Why the hell should you bother?'

'Tut, tut! Do I look so un-philanthropical? I assure you, beneath my somewhat sardonic exterior beats a romantic heart. After all, I am a poet. To continue, then. It is essential that you rapidly secure employment— remunerative employment. No: don't get angry. I am not suggesting that you embark on the commercial branch of literature in which I specialize. For that, I am sure you lack the taste and, if you'll forgive me, the talent. No—I have a better suggestion, more likely to meet with your approval.'

'The trouble is', said Henry, 'I'm not really trained to do anything.'

'This job, I suspect, requires little training, merely literacy and respectability, both of which you have in abundance. It was brought to my attention yesterday.

There is here a curious publication, in English, called *France-Miracle*. It is printed on glossy paper and sent, *gratis*, to a few thousand wealthy and important Americans every quarter. The magazine is financed by the Quai d'Orsay, and though it contains lavish articles on Paris fashions, cooking, restaurants and *objets d'art*, its main purpose is to convince the Top People in America that France is a splendidly healthy and loyal country, fully deserving of large dollops of military and economic aid, and performing an essential task in the struggle against Communism by shooting Arabs and other pawns of Krushchev. You get the drift? A propaganda sheet, pure and simple, but on a rather grandiose scale.'

'Well?'

'The publication, naturally, is supervised by the Quai d'Orsay. But it must, of course, be written by Anglo-Saxons. There is an editor, a charming Anglo-Irish baronet, somewhat down on his luck, called Sir Rupert Fitzhoward. I met him yesterday afternoon, at a cocktail-tea given to celebrate the latest issue of *Figments*, a quarterly to which I occasionally contribute. He appeared somewhat distraught. He had been obliged to dismiss his assistant, and he was, he told me, in urgent need of a replacement. Such was his distress that he even offered me the job. But I declined: I prefer to pick my own solitary way through the capitalist undergrowth. This morning, however, it occurred to me that you, in your present predicament, might be interested.'

'I am indeed', said Henry.

'The thought of undercover work for the Quai d'Orsay does not deter you? Of course not: needs must. Besides, the opportunity for sabotage may always present itself. The salary, I understand, is small but adequate. The address, which Sir Rupert kindly wrote down for me, is in the Rue de Bourgogne. Yes: here it is. I should telephone them this morning.'

'Thanks. I'm extremely grateful to you.'

'Think nothing of it. By the time you have worked in that place for a month, you will be ripe for membership of the party. And now I must be off to console Dora. She will, I think, be in a very receptive mood this morning.' Edgar slipped out from behind the table and passed rapidly through the swing-doors, leaving Henry, naturally, to pay for his coffee.

Henry lost no time in telephoning, stationing himself in the subterranean box next to the lavatory in the café. After some difficulty with the *jeton*, he dialled the number Edgar had given him.

'Hello. Can I speak to Sir Rupert, please?'

'*Comment?*' said a rude and harassed telephonist's voice.

'I want to speak to Sir Rupert Fitzhoward, please.'

'There is no such person here.' The line went dead. Irritated, Henry left the box, purchased another *jeton*, and dialled the number again.

'Hello. Sir Rupert Fitzhoward, please.'

'Pheesad? You want the *service technique?*'

'No', said Henry crossly. 'I want Sir Rupert Fitzhoward.'

'Ah—Vizard. The number is 56-67.' The line went dead again.

Henry left the box a second time, and bought three *jetons*. He dialled the second number, but there was no reply. Then he dialled the first again.

A different voice said: '*Service comptabilité.*'

'Can I speak to Sir Rupert Fitzhoward?'

'M. Hupard? One moment and I'll put you back to the operator.'

There was a click, followed by an angry buzzing, followed by a crescendo of clicks, culminating in an explosion, which almost caused Henry to jump out of the box. Then the line went dead again.

Once more Henry dialled the first number.

'*Hello*. Sir Rupert Fitzhoward, if you please.'

'M. Hupard is in conference.'

'But I don't want M. Hupard.'

'*Ecoutez, monsieur*, I have no time for conversation. Who are you trying to telephone?'

'I want the *éditeur*—I mean *rédacteur*—of *France-Miracle*.'

'Ah—Sir Fitzhoward.' There was a monumental dawning of comprehension at the other end of the line. '*Il faut le dire, monsieur*. One instant and I'll put you through.'

There was another fusillade of clicks, then absolute silence, which lasted twenty seconds.

A voice said, in English: 'Are you still there, George?'

'Is that Sir Rupert?' asked Henry.

'Of course it bloody well is! Have you got those photographs yet?'

'No—I mean, I think you're talking to the wrong person.'

'What the devil do you mean? Is that George?'

'No.'

'Then get off the bloody line.' There was a furious tapping, and once more Henry's receiver went dead.

He decided to abandon the attempt to telephone. The prospect of a job which Edgar had held out to him had never seemed very substantial; after this setback it appeared totally unreal. But Henry determined not to give up completely. He looked at the address Edgar had given him, and decided to go there in person. Sir Rupert seemed difficult, but the worst he could do would be to throw Henry out of his office.

He took a bus to the Chambre des Députés, and walked across the Place du Palais Bourbon to the Rue de Bourgogne. He found the number—a substantial, if seedy house, built over a shoeshop and a greengrocer's—and entered its dilapidated, early nineteenth century courtyard. There was no indication that *France-Miracle* was housed there and the concierge was out. A man descending the stairs told Henry that it was on the fifth floor; but this turned out to be the office of a lawyer, as Henry discovered when he had waited there ten minutes. From there he was directed to the *entresol* which proved to be some sort of bottling plant. Nobody in the bottling plant knew anything about a magazine. The house was a rambling one, with many corridors, staircases and extensions. Henry wandered through it, inspecting the nameplates on the doors, and eventually found himself at the back, overlooking a dusty garden with a willow-tree and a small statue of Mercury. Here he found a door, on which was pinned a card, scrawled in red crayon: *France-Miracle:* Editorial Enquiries. He knocked.

A voice—American, female—said: 'Come on in.'

The room was about twelve feet square, with a single window which overlooked a primitive fire-escape. There was an inner office beyond. The room was jammed with books, piles of magazines, filing cabinets and desks: three desks, to be precise. Behind two of them were young women, pounding at ancient typewriters. The third was unoccupied, and it had no chair.

One of the young women got up. She had fair hair, worn long and loose, like Alice in Wonderland, over her shoulders; a pink, childish face, and a dark blue velvet dress, tied with a white silk ribbon round her neck.

'Have you brought the photos from Agence-Vitesse?' she asked.

'No', said Henry. 'I came to see Sir Rupert.'

'Oh. Have you an appointment, please?'

'Not exactly. I—I was told there's a job going.'

'I see.' Alice in Wonderland exchanged a long look with the other girl, a round-faced brunette, who peered at Henry through thick glasses in butterfly frames. 'He's come about the job, Regina. What do *you* think?'

'I don't *know*, Francie'—her voice, too, was American —'it's difficult to tell with British'. They both looked at him silently.

'Such a sweet little grey suit', said Francie.

'And one of those adorable British ties, with smart little symbols on it.'

'Nice eyes—mmm.'

'And hands.'

'I don't like his nose. Sort of big.'

'Me neither. But the hair's cute.'

'Sure. He'll do.'

'Sure.'

Henry cleared his throat nervously. He had felt himself blushing furiously under this inspection. 'Could you tell me if I can see Sir Rupert or not?' he asked, a little sharply.

The two girls giggled. Francie said: 'You mustn't think us impolite, Mr. er——'

'Arnold. Henry Arnold.'

'Mr. Arnold. Well, I'm Francie Earle, and this is

Regina Zimovitch. She comes from Litmuss, Ohio, and I'm from Oaktown, Vermont. As I was saying, you mustn't think us impolite. You see Rupert told us to look over all the applicants, because he said that if *we* didn't like anyone then he wouldn't take them. Isn't that adorable of him?'

'No doubt', said Henry stiffly. 'I hope I met with your combined approval.'

'Check', said Francie. 'And now, if you want to see Rupert, you'll have to go to the café opposite. He does a lot of his work there, because he doesn't like the style of the furniture in his office. But we think it's because he likes to drink tea, don't we Regina?'

'Check', said Regina.

'So why don't you run along down to the Café de la Poste and see Rupert. He loves company.'

'Thanks', said Henry. Both girls looked at him solemnly as he left the room, and he heard giggles as he shut the door.

Henry found Sir Rupert without difficulty, for apart from two workmen drinking *anis*, there was only one customer in the café: tall, very English, in a charcoal grey suit, white collar and pearl grey tie. He had a long, handsome face and black hair, with distinguished touches of silver at the temples: about fifty, but fit and well-preserved. He was bending over a notebook, and on the table was a tea-cup and a large pot of tea.

'Excuse me', said Henry. 'Are you Sir Rupert Fitzhoward?'

'Yes. Have some tea. *Garçon!* Bring another cup.'

From his telephone encounter, Henry had imagined Sir Rupert would be irascible and sharp with strangers. But his voice now was mild and friendly.

'Sir Rupert, my name is Henry Arnold. I've come to see you about a job.'

'Have you now? Well, there's a job going, as it happens. Do you drink?'

'I beg your pardon?'

'Drink, my dear fellow. Alcohol, you know. Beer, whisky, gin, rum, wine, cocktails, aperitifs, liqueurs.'

Henry thought desperately. The man might be a raving teetotaller, who would not employ anyone who ever touched a drop. Or alternatively, he might have a rooted objection to teetotallers. Being an Anglo-Irishman, the latter was much more likely.

'As a matter of fact, I do have a drink occasionally.'

'I drink a lot. Quantities. Always have, all my life. It doesn't seem to have any effect, but sometimes it worries me. Does it worry you?'

'I suppose it does', said Henry cautiously 'Whenever I get—that is, on one or two occasions I've had rather too much, and then it does worry me.'

'No, I don't mean that. That's hangover. What I mean is, doesn't the thought of all the enormous quantities of drink one consumes in, say, a year, stretched out in a vast reservoir, appal you?'

'I've never thought of it that way.'

'I have, my boy. Constantly.' He picked up his note-book. 'Do you know what this is? It's a drink diary. Every morning, I write down, in detail, what I've drunk the day before. I've done it for years. Look at the entry for yesterday. A glass of wine at lunch. Two largish whiskies in my flat before dinner, while I was having a bath and shaving. Then I went to a dinner party and had another, smallish whisky before dinner. Then two fairly large-sized glasses of burgundy at dinner—I never

97

drink Champagne—and two small whiskies after dinner. Then a huge whisky when I got home as a night-cap. Does that strike you as a lot?'

'Well—'' began Henry, cautiously.

'It *is* a lot, and yet it isn't a lot. It's about normal for me. In fact a little on the light side.' He began to riffle through the pages of the notebook. 'Look, here's a bad one. Fourteen whiskies, most of a bottle of white wine and three gins before dinner. Then here's a page with a cross on it. That means I'd drunk so much that I didn't have the courage to write it down. There's always a big blank space in June or July, because that's when I go on my annual water-wagon. Three whole weeks, never miss. Done it for twenty years, and never once broke training. Do you keep a drink diary?'

'No. I'd find it rather odd to do so, I'm afraid.'

'*Odd?* My dear boy it's positively neurotic. Raving. But fascinating. I've got stacks of them at home, going back to the Thirties. They're part of one's history. You look back at them, you find your drinking habits change, subtly. For three months you drink gin-and-tonic before dinner. Then, suddenly, for no apparent reason, you switch to gin-and-bitters. Why? A broken love-affair? Or just a matter of taste? Then you find that you started drinking Campari. It lasts maybe two weeks, and then you're back on Whisky Sours. Or to go further back. In 1935, I notice, I had a passion for hock. Then in 1936, I suddenly started drinking sherry—which I loathe. Why? The Spanish Civil War, of course—I felt strongly about that. Then during the war, I notice I had nothing but rum for three weeks. Again, I hate the stuff. Why did I drink it? Shortage, of course: I was in Dungeness at the time, and the town was dry except for rum.

You've never worked on a paper before, I take it?'

'No, I'm afraid not. In fact I've never done done any job at all, unless you call being a platoon commander a job.'

'I've no idea. They made me a brigadier, and all I did was to sit in an office drinking tea. Now that's another important thing: tea. D'you like tea?'

'Yes I do, rather.'

'So do I. They can't make it here of course: they think all you have to do is to pour water on God-awful little bags full of dust. I bring my own, and make them do it properly. Lapsang Souchong, or occasionally Earl Grey. Never India or Ceylon. I have a chest brought over from Fortnum's from time to time. The great thing about tea is—never stir it. How long d'you think you should leave the tea to stand before serving?'

'I suppose about two or three minutes.'

'Wrong. Ten seconds. Never more. If the stuff then comes out too weak, it's because you haven't put enough tea in. If you want a second cup, throw the whole lot away and make another brew.'

'But that comes expensive.'

'Of course it does. Good tea *must* be expensive.' He looked at his watch. 'Good heavens—twelve already. I must dash, I'm afraid'. He stood up. Henry stood up too. He had not got the job, he had not even been interviewed for it. Sir Rupert had merely used him as a captive audience, in front of which to spout a lot of nonsense. A rising sense of anger began to sharpen Henry's disappointment.

'Goodbye', said Sir Rupert, outside the café door. 'See you this afternoon.'

'This afternoon?'

Sir Rupert looked crestfallen. 'Oh, I see. I thought you'd be able to start right away.'

'You mean I've got the job?'

'Of course, my dear fellow. I like the look of you, and the girls obviously like the look of you too, otherwise they wouldn't have sent you down here to me. But it's very annoying you can't start this afternoon.'

'But I *can* start this afternoon.'

'Then why didn't you say so before? Splendid. Be up in the office at half-past two'. He waved his hand and loped off down the Rue de Bourgogne.

Henry retired to a café by the Seine, to think things over. In a very short space of time, he had been transformed from a culture-student into a penniless down and out, and now into a journalist. Or, rather, he imagined he would be a journalist—Sir Rupert had made no reference to what sort of work he would do or, for that matter, to his salary. Having a job would mean, of course, missing all the lectures at the Sorbonne; but he could make up for it by assiduous reading in the evenings. Besides, *France-Miracle*, according to Edgar, was vaguely concerned with French culture. In any case, anything was better than returning to London.

Promptly at two-thirty, he presented himself at the office. Only Regina, the dark girl, was there, and she was in a state of panic.

'Thank goodness you've arrived at last', she said. 'Rupert's fit to be tied. He's been phoning every five minutes to ask why you hadn't come yet.'

'But he told me half-past two.'

'Did he? Oh, well, now he thinks he told you two. Don't worry. The point is, we're all in a fearful flap this afternoon because we only heard around one o'clock that we could have Zarpeg—you know, the fashion photographer. He's only free for three hours, so we've had to arrange everything frantically—models, dresses, the art people, and of course the Louvre authorities, who are terribly sticky about doing things at short notice.'

'What's it got to do with the Louvre?'

'Well, that's the theme of the series, you see. "Leading Paris couturiers show their favourite new Spring creations against the background of the masterpieces of the Louvre". The Louvre shuts, thank God, to-day, otherwise we wouldn't be able to do it at all. Francie's with Rupert now. I have to stay here to hold the fort and answer the phone. You're to jump straight into a taxi and go to the Louvre to help out.'

'But I know nothing about fashion and all that sort of thing.'

'Doesn't matter.' The phone rang. 'Lordie, that'll be Rupert again. You'd better go this instant, and I'll tell him you're already on your way.'

The taxi rattled over the Pont de la Concorde and along the Quai. At the Louvre the main entrance was very firmly shut, and Henry ran round the courtyard trying to find a side entrance. Finally, he asked a policeman—looking carefully first to see it was not the man who had pursued him a fortnight before—and was directed to a door off the Rue de Rivoli. He began to explain to the doorkeeper why he wanted to go in.

'Your documents, monsieur?'

'I have no documents, I'm afraid.'

The doorkeeper shrugged. 'Then you cannot go in. In France, you must always have documents to enter places which are officially shut.'

'But if you went inside, and asked the people in charge, they'd tell you it's all right. They know I'm coming.'

'If I went inside, monsieur, I would no longer be able to perform my function, which is to guard the door.'

'Then let me go and get them.'

'Equally, I would be failing to perform my function, for I would have allowed an unauthorized person to enter.'

'Can't we telephone to them?'

'We *can*, monsieur, but we may not. I have a telephone here, but it is used only for official business. You are unauthorized.'

'But I can pay for the call.'

'Impossible. There is nothing in the *règlement* authorizing the payment of telephone calls. This is the Louvre, monsieur, not the *Postes et Télégraphes*. We come under a different ministry.'

Henry was growing desperate. Sir Rupert had already got it into his head that he was half an hour late at the office. It was now, moreover, ten to three, and for some reason his presence was considered urgent. Should he go to a phone-box and put through a call to the head of the Louvre? Or should he phone Regina back at the office and ask for advice?

At this moment, he heard the tap of high heels on stone floor, and there was Francie.

'Thank goodness you're here at last', she said breathlessly. 'Rupert is getting frantic. Everything, but everything, is going wrong. Come on.'

'But the doorkeeper won't let me in.'

'Nonsense.' She turned on the man—a thin, wizened shrimp of officialdom in a grey overall—and subjected him to a tirade in rapid, and dazzlingly idiomatic, French. Finally, he agreed to lock the door and accompany them inside the building.

They came across Sir Rupert and his crew in the main gallery, photographing a girl in a Dior ball-dress in front of a Titian. Perched on top of a short ladder and peering through a camera on a tripod was the great Zarpeg, a short, choleric man with a huge nose and a bristling black moustache. He had taken off his coat, his shirt was unbuttoned to the waist, and sweat poured down his chest. At the foot of the ladder were his two assistants, bickering over the light-metre, which seemed to have gone wrong. Boxes of flash-bulbs, cameras, and miscellaneous apparatus were strewn about the floor. Two young women were pushing and pulling at the dress the girl was wearing, while she gazed coldly and serenely into the distance. A fat man in shirt-sleeves, whom Henry learnt was the art director of a fashion magazine, borrowed for the occasion, exchanged comments and abuse with Zarpeg. Another girl was packing a dress into a huge cardboard box. An anxious Louvre official and a bored messenger boy from Dior stood looking on. Sir Rupert paced up and down, biting his fingernails. As Henry and Francie approached, he looked up sharply.

'Has the Balmain come?' he asked Francie, ignoring Henry.

'No, Rupert. And I *told* them to send it to the Rue de Rivoli entrance.'

'Blast. We've only got one photo done in nearly an hour. The Dior's going back by their messenger. The Alsa-Marcetti's next, and that's got to be back by three-thirty at the latest—they're having a showing at four-thirty. Somebody will have to take it round immediately we've taken the photo.' He looked at Henry for the first time.

'I'm sorry there was this misunderstanding about time——' began Henry nervously.

'What the hell are you talking about? Look, here's how you can make yourself useful. As soon as we're through with the photo, grab the dress off the model and rush round with it in a taxi to Alsa-Marcetti's on the Avenue Montaigne. I'm sorry to use you as a messenger boy, but there's nobody else. Francie's got to take back the Givenchy.'

'That's quite all right', said Henry. 'You mean I have to take the dress the model's wearing now?'

'No, you fool! That's the Dior. The other model's changing into the Alsa-Marcetti now.'

There was a sudden outburst from Zarpeg at the top of his ladder.

'You moved, you bitch', he screamed at the model. 'Deliberately. I saw you.'

'I didn't', said the girl indignantly.

'Oh, for God's sake get on', said the Art Director to Zarpeg.

'How can I get on when this bitch moves just as I'm ready? She's done it three times now. Why do you employ the girl? She's notorious for it. That's why she was struck off the *Vogue* list.'

'We had to get somebody at short notice', said Sir Rupert. 'We rang up at least twenty. It's hell at this time of the year. She was the only one who was free.'

'That's not what your secretary said to me on the telephone', shouted the girl. 'She said you considered me indispensable for this assignment. She said——'

'Oh, shut up!' said Zarpeg. 'You weren't born yesterday. You weren't born this side of thirty-two years, by the look of you.'

The angelic serenity of the girl's classic, marmoreal face crumbled, and huge tears began to well down her cheeks, driving disastrous furrows through the eye-shadow.

'Now you've really done it', said the Art Director to Zarpeg. 'Why can't you keep your vulgar Hungarian mouth shut and just do your job? Now she'll have to take the dress off and put on new make-up. Look, Annette darling', he said, turning to the girl, 'M. Zarpeg's very sorry he hurt your feelings. Dry your eyes now and go off and fix yourself.'

'He hasn't *said* he's sorry', sobbed the girl. 'And my name's not Annette anyway. It's Lana.'

'I'm sorry, Lana', said Zarpeg, grinning. 'Now run along and be good.'

'Look', said Sir Rupert. 'While we're waiting, let's do the Alsa-Marcetti in front of the Mona Lisa. Incidentally, where the hell is Cleo? She should be ready by now. Go and get her, Francie.'

The floods, arc-lights, camera and ladder were laboriously trundled down the gallery and positioned round the Mona Lisa. Zarpeg demanded that the velvet curtains behind the painting be removed, but the Louvre official, outraged, refused. Zarpeg then refused to take the photograph. A heated argument began to develop.

'Why not take it in front of another painting?' asked Henry.

'Brilliant', said Sir Rupert. 'That tatty old Mona Lisa is frightfully old hat, anyway. Let's try Raphael's *Young Man With a Glove*. The Alsa-Marcetti will stand out well against the black.'

Once more the lights and the camera were moved. Henry, who had been transporting and erecting Zarpeg's ladder, looked up to find Francie had returned with the second model, Cleo.

On one occasion, at school, Henry had received a heavy blow on the head during a rugger match. There was no blood, he was not concussed, and he continued to play. But he lost his memory. The sensation was bewildering, but not unpleasant. For a few minutes, he did not know who or where he was, or what he was supposed to be doing. He walked around in a trance, conscious he was still alive, but equally conscious that he was inhabiting a dream world. When memory returned, and with it knowledge of the world around him, Henry was relieved, of course, but also a little regretful: his experience of mental disembodiment—the only way he could describe it—had had a touch of magic to it.

As soon as he saw Cleo, Henry relived this experience. The gallery, the old masters, Zarpeg and his cameras, Sir Rupert, the Art Director, Francie and the girls, the official and the messenger boy—all disappeared from his mind. His eyes saw them; but his mind did not register what his eyes saw. The only object which it could comprehend was Cleo, as she stood, adjusting her dress, six feet away.

Seen across a room, Cleo might have been dismissed as a very ordinary pretty girl. Her hair was black, full, and shone with the dark brilliance of polished Caucasian marble; but black hair, when all is said and done, has its limitations. Her eyebrows were slim, perfect arches—but then so many are, or can be made to be. Her blue eyes, too, were nothing out of the ordinary, though clear, and the colour of the Adriatic on a sharp October morning. Her features were classical—but such as could be found on five thousand models from Park Avenue to the Via Veneto—and only the warm, wide mouth gave a hint of generosity rarely to be found in the species. Her figure, too, was a little fuller than usual, and served to bring out the ranging contours of the ivory watered-silk dress she wore; but again, in all essentials, it was a figure of average perfection. What made Cleo beautiful, what transcended all these features and combined them into a living miracle of breathless joy to behold, was the dazzling brilliance of her skin.

English women are usually credited with the finest skins in the world, and the proposition is true, if we take the nation as a whole; American girls, especially those from the deep south, often possess rosy marble skins, but they are easily destroyed by sun and wind; and many Venetian women, too, have skins of soft, pale fragility, particularly if they are tall and have red hair. The skins of Frenchwomen, by contrast, tend to be dull and muddy, tolerable only when they are burnt brown or black by the Riviera sun. But there are a few French-women—a very, very few, and always with some foreign blood—who have skins of a positive beauty to be found nowhere else. They are not white or pink, but very pale gold, and they appear to radiate an inner light through the smooth opaqueness of the flesh. Such a skin cannot be ruined by sun: it merely deepens and intensifies the light, turning it from gold to amber. Cleo's skin was of this kind, and it made her a bad model, for it turned the ivory silk—the best that Lyons could make—into something cheap and shallow.

Cleo has been described through the eye of one particular beholder. It may be that others would have been less impressed or found more faults. But this is irrelevant to the story. Henry, at any rate, was quite overwhelmed. He was not a romantic young man, and had certainly never been in love. His attitude towards women was compounded of fear, desire, the post-adolescent's wish to conquer, and pessimism as to the likelihood of success. These varied greatly with the appearance of the woman —desire, being purely sexual, remaining static, but fear and pessimism increasing in direct proportion to the quality of her looks. Women occupied a good deal of his thoughts, though the pursuit of any particular one had never dominated his life. But at the sight of Cleo, his usual complex of responses were swept away and replaced by one paramount emotion, which he could not attempt to analyse, but was something approaching what he felt when he gazed on a great masterpiece of art. It was not love—or not yet love—because you cannot love the Sistine *Madonna*, or Van Eyck's *Altarpiece at Ghent* or Donatello's *David*; it was astonished adoration.

Henry must have looked at Cleo for a full ten seconds, before Zarpeg's crêpe-soled suede boot descended heavily on his left hand, which was holding a rung of the step-ladder. He swore, and this brought an answering expletive, in Low Hungarian, from Zarpeg.

'Children, children', said the Art Director, a plump, feminine creature, fond of peace and beauty. 'Let's get on for pity's sake. Cleo, darling, stand just to the left of the young man in the painting. That's right. The left hand *thus*. The hem of the dress *thus*. The right arm follows the line of the young man's arm *thus*.' He scurried back behind the camera, and cocked his round head from one side to the other.

'A very vulgar pose', said Sir Rupert. 'But then Americans like vulgarity.'

'*I* like vulgarity', said the Art Director. 'Beautiful, beautiful vulgarity. Lobster salad, pink champagne, strawberry-coloured Cadillacs, Renoir, Saint-Saëns, Paul de Kok, Ava Gardner, Balmain——'

'Tinned salmon', said Cleo. 'I like to eat tinned salmon and drink double martinis sitting on a Second Empire sofa and reading *Dimanche-Matin*.'

'I like', said Francie slowly, 'drinking double choco-late ice-cream sodas with a jigger of vodka in them, and reading *Mademoiselle*.'

'Seven-Up and Framboise', said Sir Rupert. 'That's the most vulgar drink I know.'

'Have you ever tried Asti-Spumante and pineapple juice', said Henry, 'mixed with shaved ice?'

'It sounds delicious', said Cleo, looking at him for the first time. 'You must make me one.'

Henry felt himself blushing in a positively terrifying manner, at thus being the direct centre of Cleo's attentions. His predicament, indeed, might have been obvious, but at that moment, Zarpeg, who had been fiddling about behind his camera and muttering at his assistants, exploded in a fresh outburst of rage.

'Gentlemen, it is quite impossible for me to take this photo.'

The others looked at him, silently. Sir Rupert lit a cigarette, bringing a despairingly ineffectual glance of reproach from the Louvre official.

'Gentlemen, do you hear—I cannot take this photo'. His voice had risen a pitch. 'Why do you not ask me why?'

'Well, why?' asked Sir Rupert.

'Because I cannot photograph fat women. Your model

is too fat. She is bursting out of that dress. She is a fat female camel. Moreover, her skin is dreadful—it ruins the dress. Models should have white skins. This girl is a cannibal.'

'Now look here——' began Henry involuntarily.

'Shut up', said Sir Rupert to Henry sharply.

'Dammit, sir', said Henry hotly, in his best sixth-form manner, 'one can't allow that chap to insult a girl——'

'Shut up', said Sir Rupert. 'Leave this to me'. He turned to Zarpeg. 'Look here, Zarpeg, I've had just about enough of you this afternoon. You're paid—and handsomely paid, too—to come here and take photographs, not to criticize the models. Let me finish, blast you!'—his voice rang out in commanding tones: there was a touch of his arrogant Anglo-Irish ancestors in Sir Rupert when roused. 'You've already wasted half-an-hour by upsetting the other girl. Cleo's not supposed to be a professional model. She's only come here to oblige me at the last moment.'

'So I, Zarpeg, am expected to photograph amateurs?'

'You'll photograph what you're bloody well told to. You think you're big time, don't you? But I'll have you put on every black list in Paris. This set-up this afternoon is already costing my paper 300,000 francs. Right. You walk out now, and I'll make sure every fashion editor in the city knows it by this evening—*Vogue, Harpers, Album de Figaro, Elle*——'

'I refuse to discuss anything under threats', said Zarpeg stiffly, beginning to descend the ladder.

'The point is academic', said Cleo. Everyone turned to look at her. 'I said I liked vulgar things. I *detest* vulgar men. I refuse to be photographed by this counter-jumping *parvenu*.'

'Children, children', said the Art Director, rolling his eyes in despair.

'You heard what she said?' screamed Zarpeg, turning on him. 'She refuses to be photographed by me. It is inadmissible.'

'Your moustache is vulgar', said Cleo remorselessly. 'Your shoes are vulgar, you use vulgar hair-oil—ugh—your accent is vulgar, you have a nose like a potato, your breath smells of cheap pernod——' She turned to the assembled company. 'How can I possibly allow myself to be photographed by this Hungarian peasant?'

'You cannot *not* be photographed by me', said Zarpeg. 'I do not work with ultimatums. I may be vulgar—I do not dispute it. I come from the soil—yes, and proud of it. But I have talent, mademoiselle, talent such as you and your high-born ancestors could never possess in a million years! Talent admits no refusals. You will *submit* your body to being photographed!'

'Look', said Sir Rupert, drily, 'let's get on with the photograph'.

Zarpeg clambered back up the ladder; Cleo resumed her pose. For twenty minutes there was virtual silence. Then, after the final flash, Zarpeg looked up.

'Excellent, excellent, *mademoiselle*. We shall have a marvellous plate here.'

'Right', said Sir Rupert. 'Cleo, get that dress off as quickly as you can. Francie, go and give her a hand'. They scurried off, the silk whispering over the marble floor.

'Now for the Dior, if the other wretched creature's ready', said Sir Rupert, 'and for God's sake, Zarpeg, keep a civil tongue in your head.' He turned round, and saw Henry. 'Well, what the bloody hell do you think you're doing? Go and get Cleo's dress and take it back to Alsa-Marcetti! The girls will help you to pack it.'

'But she's changing', protested Henry.

'Then give her a hand.'

'But *really*——'

'Haven't you ever seen a girl changing before? This isn't a prep-school. There'll be hell to pay if that dress arrives too late for the afternoon presentation. Well, *move*!'

Henry ran down the gallery, and into the small alcove where Cleo was changing. She was already stepping out of the swirling folds of silk as he arrived, and he caught a confused glimpse of long, golden limbs and lace underclothes.

'Ah, here's Henry,' said Francie indistinctly, her mouth full of pins. 'I do believe the boy's blushing.'

Cleo grinned at him, as she struggled into a grey flannel skirt. 'That's the first healthy blush I've seen on a young man's face for simply ages.' She spoke excellent English, though she put a French emphasis on the words.

'Look', said Henry to Francie, to avoid looking at Cleo, 'I've got to take this dress to Alsa-Marcetti or something. Where is it?'

'I've got my car', said Cleo, buttoning the coat of her suit over her brassiere. 'I'll take you. I'm going home to Passy and it's on my way.'

'Thanks', said Henry. He could feel himself begin to blush again, and buried his face in the folds of the dress which he and Francie were stuffing into a huge, black, glossy box. His luck seemed to be in; a ride in Cleo's car was unhoped-for bliss. But he must be careful. Cleo was so far beyond his range as to be quite unattainable; and she provoked in him responses which were quite new to him, and for which he was completely unprepared. At all costs he must not make a fool of himself.

Cleo ran lightly out of the Louvre, Henry staggering behind with his box. She had parked her car—a tiny, shining Renault—in the Rue de Rivoli at a strictly forbidden time and place, and a minatory policeman was standing over it. At the sight of Cleo, however, he straightened up, smiled broadly, and flourished a handsome salute.

'Thanks', said Cleo, unlocking the car. 'So sweet of you to look after it.'

'A pleasure, *mademoiselle*.'

They roared off up the street, Cleo manipulating the gears with grinding abandon.

'I think you were illegally parked', said Henry.

'Was I? *Really*. Oh, dear, that explains why the policeman was there. Fortunately he knew me. That's why he let me off, I suppose. You mustn't think that French policemen do that to every pretty girl. But perhaps you don't think I am pretty anyway.'

'Yes, I do.'

'Good. So you don't agree with what that horrid photographer said. But of course you don't—you protested. That was nice of you.'

'Not at all.'

'As a matter of fact, what he said was true—up to a point, anyway. I'm too fat to model. A model has to be such a wraith, you know. As they say, you can always add it on with padding, but you can't take it off. A good model should have thirty-two-inch hips at the most. Mine are thirty-four. But then I don't want to be a model.'

'I don't like models, much.'

'Nor do I. They get no fun, poor dears, no nice food and drinks and lying in the sun. It turns them inward, and then all they think about is me, me, me. Rather boring for men, I should have thought, but they seem to like it.'

Crossing the Place de la Concorde, Cleo fell silent, hanging grimly over the wheel to avoid the swirling maelstrom of cars. Henry was silent, too. He was longing desperately to ask Cleo if she would meet him for a drink; but he knew he would not dare. And in a few fleeting seconds, they were across the Champs Elysées and in the Avenue Montaigne. The car jerked to a stop outside a silk awning, between two vast, plate-glass windows.

Henry wanted to say something significant, as he got out, grasping his box. But all he could manage was: 'Thanks very much.'

'Goodbye', said Cleo, slamming the door. The car shot off, leaving nothing behind but a thin trail of blue exhaust smoke. On this banal exchange, Cleo had passed out of his life, and he had not made even the most timid gesture to retain her. He didn't even know her full name. She had seemed to like him, but her curt 'Goodbye' had made it quite clear that he was just a tiny incident in a life glittering with glamour and drama; she had probably forgotten him before even she reached the Alma-Marceau. Henry turned round sadly towards the Maison Alsa-Marcetti.

There are literally thousands of dress-shops in Paris: scruffy ateliers in the Rue Montmartre, dowdy shops around the Rue de Babylon selling dresses copied from photographs in the *Album de Figaro* or *L'Officiel*, pseudo-smart shops in the Champs Elysées, third-floor flats in the XV arrondissement, where young, slender men with talent and no money are trying to break into the trade; shops of all sizes, tastes and price. But there is only a handful of giants, whose commands change the women of the world. Nearly all of them are in the graceful network of broad avenues north of the Alma-Marceau. There is the house Dior created. It no longer rules so absolutely, but it is still powerful: size, range, money, the fabulous quality of its silks and cottons and cloths, its superb team of cutters and seamstresses—the finest in the history of fashion—keep it in the race. There is Balmain, who has taken the place of Fath, and creates the spectacular, the opulent and the magisterial (if Queen Elizabeth bought her dresses in Paris, which unfortunately she doesn't, she would probably choose Balmain). There is the sly, ingenious Coco Chanel, who has been designing the same, simple pastel dresses for years, and so enabling wealthy women of forty to look ten years younger. There is Castillo, of Lanvin-Castillo, who sculpts delicate patterns and rich fabrics in the Chinese style, and is a godsend to ugly millionairesses. There is Balenciaga, the man whom all *couturiers* regard as their leader, whose line is classic and unchanging, who scorns to sell his *toiles* to the all-powerful American buyers, and who creates individual masterpieces which the richest women in the world are proud to wear. There is Givenchy, the tall young man whom many believe will eventually take Balenciaga's place; an individualist, too, who has created a generation of coltish, Audrey Hepburn young women. And, above all, there is Alsa-Marcetti, the great house, founded by Madame Alsa, which enshrines the talents of Cosimo Marcetti. Surly, saturnine, silent, Marcetti now sets the Paris line, as once Dior did. But he is never photographed, his château near

Dijon is closely guarded, and only a few privileged clients ever see him. The business is run by his chief, indispensible and formidable assistant, Madame Opal.

Henry pushed through the glass swing-door, gilded with fleurs-de-lis, and trod into the thick, sky-bluecarpet of the reception floor of the salon. The room was heavily scented with the famous Alsa-Marcetti 'Ambassadrice'. There were a few gilt chairs, a sofa covered in yellow silk, pastoral scenes by Marie Laurencin on the walls. A sales-girl in a tight black dress glided forward, and Henry handed her the box.

'It's from *France-Miracle*, mademoiselle', he said.

'In that case, monsieur, you cannot hand it to me. All the dresses we lend to be photographed must be returned personally to Madame Opal! Will you follow me?'

They entered a small and fragile lift, rather like the gilded cage of a parrot, and shot up two floors. Here was the ante-room to the main salon, and already black-clad girls were moving chairs ready for the afternoon presentation of the collection. Madame Opal entered with a magisterial swish of black silk and a rattle of amber beads. Short and plump, she bore some resemblance to the proprietress of the Café Zok: the red gash of the lips, the rouged cheeks, the black, unsympathetic hair were the same; but there was an imperious light in her steel-grey eyes which Madame Gobat could never have equalled. She was also in a towering rage.

'At last', she said, bearing down on Henry. 'You return this dress. Do you know what time it is? Ten minutes to four. I was given an absolute promise that the dress would be returned at three-thirty at the latest.'

'I'm very sorry', said Henry. 'We had trouble taking the photos.'

'Trouble? What do I care about your troubles? How can I present our collection at four-thirty if all the dresses are scattered over Paris? You should think of *my* troubles.'

'I'm sorry', said Henry. 'Good afternoon, madame.' He turned to go.

'Oh no, you don't', screamed Madame Opal. 'Stop him, Françoise. You don't leave, young man, until I've inspected the dress. I know you magazine people.' She hurled off the lid of the box and began to rummage in the tissue-paper.

'I thought so', she explained with a yelp of angry triumph. 'Pigs! Savages! Look at this dress—it's ruined, ruined!' She lifted it in armfuls from the box and flourished it under Henry's nose. He gazed at it abjectly.

'What do you have as models—elephants? Rhinoceroses? Look at this seam—here—it's beginning to come apart. And here, too! And what's this? *Sweat.* Your model is a fat sweaty girl, and she is not fit to wear a dress by Alsa-Marcetti. Look—it is discoloured——'

'I'm sorry', repeated Henry desperately, 'I'm sure——'

'What do I care for your sorrow?' said Madame Opal. 'What about my dress? Look—the skirts are crushed. It will have to be ironed. And then what happens to the finish on the silk? Eh? Answer me!'

'I have no idea.'

'Then I will give you an idea. Take that!' Before Henry could duck, Madame Opal had dealt him a powerful box on the ear with the flat of her broad, bejewelled hand. He was preparing to defend himself against a second when one of the assistants intervened.

'Madame Opal, please! He is only the messenger-boy.'

'I am not a messenger-boy', said Henry indignantly.

'You see?' shouted Madame Opal. 'He is not a messenger-boy. He is responsible with his sweaty, elephant models.' She lunged forward at him again, and this time two of the assistants had to restrain her by putting their slim arms round her ample waist. Henry, heart thumping, dodged back into the lift, slammed the gilded door, and pressed the button. A sound of high feminine voices, raised in argument, came from above. Henry walked briskly through the ground-floor room—he would really have liked to run—and found the girl who had directed him to the lift giggling. He shot her an angry glance and plunged out of the glass door.

It was now four o'clock. Henry supposed he had better return to the Louvre. He ran down to the end of the Avenue and hailed a taxi. They were immediately wedged in a traffic-jam, which spread out all along the river to the Concorde. By the time Henry reached the Louvre, and had argued his way past the doorkeeper again, the party from *France-Miracle* was packing up. Sir Rupert had gone.

'Look here', said Henry to Francie, 'something frightful's happened about the dress.'

Francie laughed. 'Did you meet the terrible Ogress Opal?'

'I certainly did. She said the dress was ruined, and then she began a positive physical assault on me.'

'Oh dear—I should have warned you. She always behaves like that. She tried to scratch my face once. The dress is perfectly all right. Don't give it another thought.'

'Well, the next time Sir Rupert wants a dress returned, he can do it himself.'

'Not him—he's much too scared of the Opal. He's off to his girl-friend for consolation after his harrowing afternoon. She's a coal-black Berber girl from Marrakesh who dances at the Cocotte.'

'Oh', said Henry. 'Then what am I supposed to do now? Nobody's even explained to me what my job is.'

'I will. But it's too complicated to do today, because I have to rush to catch the shops. Just go home now, and have a nice drink.'

Henry strolled over from the Louvre, across the Pont du Carrousel, and on to the Left Bank. He sat down at a café overlooking the river, and ordered himself a large *fine à l'eau*. He had a lot to think about.

# IV

HENRY began work in earnest at *France-Miracle* the next morning. When he arrived, at nine-thirty, Regina was already installed behind her typewriter, and Francie was sticking up proofs with scissors and paste.

She flashed Henry one of her little-girl smiles. 'Take your coat off, Henry—I may call you Henry, mayn't I?—and I'll show you how it's done.' Henry dragged over a chair and sat down beside her.

'You see, we get in the manuscripts, and then Regina types them to our specification. Then Rupert chooses the type and M. Pomphot—he's the Art Director you met yesterday—sends over the lay-outs with the photos marked, and we send the stuff down to the printers. They're all French, you know, so it comes back full of mistakes, and we correct them. Then I stick up the galleys on the dummy lay-out like this—see?—and then we send it back. Sometimes the page-proofs come back rather goofy, so we have to fix them again. Then Rupert sort-of *considers* them—he's very artistic you know—and if he doesn't quite like them, he makes squiggles all over, and then the printers start complaining and it gets time for us to go to press, and finally Rupert marks all the pages *bon à tirer*—that means good to draw, literally, I don't know how you'd say it in English, technically I mean—and we go to press and that's all'. She paused for breath.

'You forgot to explain the different types of paper', said Regina.

'Oh yes, thank you, Regina. Well, I don't really understand this bit myself, you see, but there are different types of paper in the magazine. One's called *typopresse*, and that's easy because there are no complications at all. And another's called *couleur*, and that's rather complicated because there are two proofs of each page, and they're not quite the same—I don't exactly know why.'

'*I* do', said Regina. 'It's because one proof is for the black ink and another for the colour. They go in separately.'

'But there are four colours, Regina. And they don't, they go in together.'

'They do too go in separately—I saw them do it when that cute little man with a glass eye showed me round the printing works. I think there's a different press for each colour.'

'There isn't. Anyway it doesn't matter. The point is, there are two proofs, and we have to make them the same.'

'Then there's offset', said Regina. 'You've forgotten that.'

'I hadn't. I was coming to it. Offset is on rough paper, and it's sort of printed on a film and then engraved on a cylinder.'

'No. It's engraved on a stone. It's the same as lithograph.'

'Please, Regina, I'm supposed to be doing the explaining. Then there's photogravure. That's the same as offset, only somewhat different.'

'How different?' asked Henry, who was listening with growing alarm to this catalogue of obscure complexities.

'Well, it's printed on different sort of paper, to begin with. Rather greyish.'

'It's a process', said Regina portentously, 'for printing at great speed. A proof of the text and photograph is made into a negative transparency, which is transferred by means of a photo-electric cell to a copper cylinder.'

'I'm sure that bit about a photo-electric cell can't be right', said Henry.

'Of course it isn't', said Francie. 'Don't listen to her, Henry dear. She's just picked up a few technical phrases from her boy-friend on *Paris-Match*. Anyway, none of this matters. We just correct the proofs, and there's a sort of miraculous process at the printers that turns everything into a magazine. That is', she added doubtfully, 'when everything goes all right.'

'Some qualification', said Regina grimly.

'Yes', said Francie. 'From time to time something goes wrong, and the printers start telephoning angrily and Rupert gets *furious*, and we get what he calls rockets. I do think that's one of your cutest English phrases.'

'I see', said Henry. 'And what am I supposed to do?'

'Oh, you just generally supervise me.'

'But don't supervise her too much', said Regina meaningfully. 'The last guy we had did, and he had to go, didn't he Francie?'

Francie shook back her long golden locks. Henry noticed that, despite her pink-and-white complexion, *ingénue* clothes, and generally girlish appearance, there were tiny lines at the corners of her eyes and mouth. He guessed she was thirty (she was thirty-five, actually).

'Well', she said, 'he would keep on making passes at me.'

'Francie's a dyke, aren't you, Francie?'

'Really, Regina——'

'A dyke?' asked Henry. 'What's a dyke?' The girls

exchanged glances and giggled. Henry felt himself blushing again.

'Apart from supervising', he went on hurriedly, 'what do I have to do?'

'Nothing, really. Oh, yes. You have to look at the manuscripts when they come in, and correct the grammar. Rupert says we girls aren't clever enough to do that. He says American girls aren't educated in their colleges.'

'Check', said Regina. 'All I ever learnt was taught me by my Jewish grandmother, and she spoke with a Yiddish accent.'

'All right', said Henry, 'correct grammar. Anything else?'

'Oh yes', said Francie, 'I forgot the most important thing of all. *You* have to look after Madame Plympton-La Fouette.'

'Really?' asked Henry. 'And what does that involve?'

'Trouble', said Regina.

'Not necessarily. She might like him. She liked Mr. Benbow, who was the one before your predecessor. Rupert says it was because she was having an *affaire* with him, but I don't believe it for one instant. I think she just had a motherly affection for him because he was so young and reminded her of her kid brother.'

'Oh yeah?' said Regina. 'And that, I suppose, is why she always asked him to call and collect her copy *personally*, always towards the end of the afternoon, when Monsieur le Comte was safely away in his girl-friend's flat in Chantilly.'

'Regina, your coarseness disgusts me.'

'But who *is* this woman?' asked Henry anxiously.

'Madame la Comtesse Plympton-La Fouette', said

Francie. 'She's American—only daughter of Silas Plympton, the Dallas haberdashery tycoon. La Fouette is a rather crummy aristocrat, who plays around with right-wing politics. He married her for her money. She married him for his title. They entertain a lot—she's reckoned the leading political hostess here. Taxim—that's the Quai d'Orsay official who keeps an eye on us all—is very much on a string.'

'Unfortunately', said Regina, 'she fancies herself as a newspaperwoman.'

'And that's where we come in', said Francie. 'She does us a column about the political scene here. You know—"I was talking to my old friend M. Bidault the other day, and he said——" It's pretty basic, I'm afraid. What you have to do is to take it from her tiny hand, put it into ordinary English, and then square it with her. The trouble is, Claudel, who probably couldn't read a word of English anyway, once told her she had an elegant prose style, so she's a bit sensitive about what is done to her copy. So go easy with the blue pencil. Otherwise, M. Taxim is liable to send round one of his memorandums.'

'Memoranda,' said Henry instinctively.

'O.K.—I'm firmly back in my transatlantic inferiority status. I can see you and the Plympton will get along just fine. Anyway, cast that roving grammatical eye of yours over her latest gem. It's right here.'

She handed Henry a few untidy sheets of paper, and Henry sat down at his desk to read them. They were typewritten, but many phrases were scratched out and scrawled over in an uneven, childish hand. A sentence caught his eye: 'The only thing wrong with this country is that there are too many Communists in it.' Another read: 'Washington is grossly misinformed about the situation in Algeria. America must support France in Algeria, because otherwise the Arab Communists will take over Africa.' Originally, '. . . and Asia' had been added, but this was crossed out. From his brief perusal, Henry gathered that Madame Plympton-La Fouette's views were inclined to the Right.

The door slammed open, and Sir Rupert strode in, swinging an ebony, silver-knobbed cane. He looked at Henry with astonishment, then remembered, and nodded distantly.

'Have the proofs of the Corbusier article arrived?' he snapped at Francie.

'On your desk, Rupert.'

'And Helbert?'

'He called half an hour ago. I told him we'd take the Coty reportage.'

'What about Zarpeg?'

'His assistant called. The transparencies will be round this afternoon.'

'Taxim?'

'He wants some sentences changed in the piece about Franco-German relations.'

'Blast. Why can't he make up his mind sooner? Call Heurot at the printers and tell him to hold the offset folio. Regina, get the changes from Taxim, hop into a taxi and copy them out at the printers.' He jerked his thumb at Henry. 'What's he doing?'

'Reading the Plympton.'

'That's good'. He turned to Henry. 'You get into the good books of that woman, my boy—it's as much as your job is worth if you don't. I don't care what you do with her copy as long as it's English and she's happy. But I warn you: don't argue with her about politics—she knows less about them than you do, and that's dangerous. Your predecessor made that particular mistake. And above all, remember one thing: don't come to me about her. I will have nothing whatsoever to do with that woman. She's poison in m'blood. Understand?'

'Yes, sir', said Henry.

'And don't call me sir. Call me Rupert, Fitzhoward, anything you like, but don't make me think I'm back in the army.' He turned to Francie. 'Anything else?'

'A Madame Forceau wants you to dine with her Thursday.'

'Tell her no. And if a Madame Offlous telephones, tell her I'm in Menton. If a Madame La Cassasse telephones, put her straight through.'

He banged into his office, slamming the door.

'He's in his executive mood this morning, the darling,' said Francie. 'Probably to impress you. Normally, he doesn't want to know about these things—we muddle through ourselves in our own way. Oh, and that reminds me of another thing: never show him an article or ask his opinion about one. He hates reading. I don't believe he's read a single article since I've been here. So long as Taxim says they're O.K. politically, and you pass them for grammar, he's happy.'

'What an extraordinary man. He hasn't even told me whether I've been definitely hired, or whether I'm on trial, or even what my salary is.'

'You're hired all right. He obviously likes you—in fact I bet he'll soon creep out, meek and mild as anything and not executive at all, and suggest you go across the road for some tea.'

'But I don't understand him at all. Why is he doing this job?'

'He won't go back to England any more. He was involved in a terrible row when he was in the army. He had an affair with the young wife of a general, and was court-martialled. He seems to have lost all his money, too. So a friend of his—he moves around in high society here, you know—got him this job, and he seems to like it.'

'Don't worry about your salary', said Regina. It's 50,000 francs a month. Paid in arrears, at the end of the month. Actually, starting now, you probably won't get paid until the end of next month.'

'Oh', said Henry. 'That's a bore.'

'Do you want to borrow money?' asked Francie. 'I can lend you 30,000 if you like.'

'Well, really', said Henry, 'it's very kind of you, but the fact is—or rather, as a matter of fact, I might want to take you up on that in a week or so. The point is, that's why I've taken this job, you see——'

'Don't bother to explain. I know what it's like to be in Paris without any money. Are you sure you wouldn't like some now? He doesn't look as though he gets enough to eat, does he, Regina?'

'Kind of peaky.'

'Please', said Henry, 'I'm perfectly all right for the moment——'

The telephone rang. Francie picked it up. 'It's for you, Henry. The secretariat of Madame Plympton calling.' She handed him the receiver.

'Hello', he said.

'This is Madame la Comtesse Plympton-La Fouette's senior secretary speaking', said a very American female voice. 'Madame would like to know whether her article has been finalized for printing.'

'I'm doing it at the moment.'

'Good. Madame would like you to bring it round this afternoon about three, so she can check it over.'

'I suppose I can', said Henry dubiously.

'Pardon?'

Henry saw the two girls frantically signalling to him and nodding their heads.

'I mean, of course I will', he said. 'Thank you very much,' he added lamely.

'You're welcome', said the secretary, ringing off.

'That's the stuff', said Francie. 'Always keep on the right side of the old girl.'

'I thought authors came to see editors, and not vice-versa', said Henry.

'La Plympton is not an author—she's a millionairess. And don't you ever forget it, if you want to stay around here.'

Sir Rupert remained in his office all morning, though quite what he was doing neither Henry nor the girls knew. He appeared to run the paper by remote control, only descending to points of actual editorial detail in occasional moments of furious activity—as when he had presided over the taking of the photographs the day before. His quiescence, however, enabled Henry to get on with editing Madame Plympton's copy. This was a formidable task: the Countess' schooling, as Francie explained, had taken place at a period when Plympton Senior was still making his first five hundred dollars, and had therefore been perfunctory. By lunchtime, Henry was still hard at work.

At ten to one, Sir Rupert came out of his office beaming. He paused over Henry's desk. 'That's the stuff, Charles. Teach the old girl she can't put "i" before "e" except after "c", eh? Well, I'm off. I have just devised a new scheme for promoting Franco-American unity, which I shall present to friend Taxim this afternoon. So I shan't be coming back. Francie, all callers are to be told I'm in conference.' He swept out of the door.

'I know', said Francie, 'he's going racing at St. Cloud.'

'Sure', said Regina. 'And that's why he's been so quiet all morning—studying form.'

'He doesn't even seem to know my name', complained Henry.

'Probably not', said Francie. 'He never learnt your predecessor's. I worked here for six months before he stopped calling me Alice.'

'It's all very depressing. I'm not even sure whether I'm really employed here.'

'Don't worry. I phoned the *service comptabilité* this morning and had you registered. They're the only people who matter, because they run the payroll.'

'Thanks', said Henry. He went back to his labours on Madame Plympton. The girls left for lunch, leaving him still at it, and it was not until nearly two that he felt himself satisfied. By this time the original typesheet was a spider's web of excisions, arrows and balloons. He put it on top of Regina's desk for retyping, and went out to get a sandwich. The first person he saw in the street was Crick. There was no avoiding him: they met face to face, and Henry's first instinct was to adopt a defensive posture. But Crick's mood seemed to be shifty rather than aggressive.

'Hello, Arnold', he said. 'Unfortunate, that dust-up we had the other night.'

E

'Yes. I see you're out of gaol.'

Crick grinned. 'Well, you know old boy, Dora raised the cash somehow. Don't ask me how. What are you doing here?'

'I work here.'

'Really. That's interesting. What at, might I ask?'

'It's none of your business, but as a matter of fact I'm on the editorial staff of a paper called *France-Miracle*.'

'I know, old boy. Saw a copy once in the Biltmore Hotel, New York City. Classy job. My congratulations.'

'Thanks. And now I must go.'

'Just a second, old feller. You wouldn't like to lend me a few thousand francs, would you? Just for old time's sake.'

'No.'

'O.K. I just asked. I'll be seeing you.'

'Probably not.' Henry walked past him, rather self-consciously declining to respond to Crick's wave of the hand. He very much doubted that Crick had forgiven him for the affray at the Rhumerie de Guadeloupe. His superficial amiability had been dictated by his need for money. Since that had been refused, he could expect trouble from Crick if their paths crossed again.

However, he had no time to worry about Crick. After a hasty sandwich, he dashed back to the office, and found Regina already pounding out the revised version of Madame Plympton's article. It was a quarter to three by the time she had finished, and Henry immediately snatched it and dashed by taxi to the Plympton-La Fouette residence in Passy.

It was, as he had expected, of some magnificence. Madame Plympton had bought two adjoining nine-teenth-century houses, knocked them down, and erected in their place a neo-classical monstrosity, set back from the road, and guarded by high walls, gilded gates and a gate-house. Here Henry was stopped by a uniformed attendant, and asked his business. On being told, the attendant telephoned through to the house, about fifty yards away. Only then was Henry escorted to the front door, which was opened by a white-coated butler.

'Madame la Comtesse has told me to put you in the Blue salon', he said. 'She will be down presently.'

The Blue salon contained, on Henry's rough calculation, just over one hundred pieces of furniture, mainly Louis Quinze. The walls were hung in blue silk, and adorned with three Renoirs, a Picasso, a Cézanne *Mont St. Victoire*, a Dufy, two Monets, and a self-portrait by Van Gogh. On the mantlepiece, which was about fourteen feet in length, there was a sprinkling of Chinese jade figures, tiny Byzantine ikons, and a classical Greek figurine which Henry had seen reproduced in an illustrated book about Greek art. There were cabinets loaded with Sèvres, Meissen, Renaissance Majolica and Dresden. Only the carpet was modern: for not even Madame Plympton's wealth could persuade Persian craftsmen to make a carpet more than an inch thick, and this was almost two. It was like walking on a velvet swamp. Henry sat down gingerly on a Louis Seize upright armchair with bronze *pieds de sphinx* which had once belonged to the Prince de Talleyrand.

Madame Plympton's entrance was abrupt and spectacular. Henry had kept his eyes fixed on the double doors through which he had been escorted by the butler, ready to rise as soon as the great lady should appear. Instead, he heard a soft whirring behind him, turned round, and saw that a section of the silk-covered wall had slid back, revealing a diminutive lift, from which stepped five foot nine inches of middle-aged Texan womanhood, arrayed in the most fearsome war-paint which the entire Paris glamour industry could provide.

All those who knew Honor Plympton at all well despised her. But they were all prepared to concede her one thing: she got the most out of her money. Most millionaires live private lives of dedicated anxiety; Honor Plympton rattled her money in people's faces and laughed at their startled expressions. She did, said, ate, drank and wore exactly what she wished. If a man—or a woman—had a price, she paid it; if not, she passed on: she had no use for anything not based on a calculable cash nexus. This attitude horrified many, but it also had a certain residual honesty about it. With her, you knew exactly where you were, right from the start.

Madame Plympton's habit of laying her cards face down on the table was reflected in her appearance. Tall and big-boned, but without the covering of flesh to give her body any voluptuous appeal, she could fairly be described as ungainly; and her face, with its wide, coarse mouth, big straight nose and small grey eyes, was distinctly plain. Given this, there was only one way to impose herself on the world: and that was to shock—a strategy she carried out with devastating thoroughness. Her hair, long and thick but originally of an indeterminate colour, was dyed canary yellow and piled in rich, creamy curls on top of her head. Her face was a mask of eye-shadow and rouge, the lips yawning like the red-slashed mouth of a pillar-box, the eyes concealed behind dark butterfly-glasses, rimmed with tiny diamonds, in each corner of which a monstrous and icy sapphire glittered. Around her throat was a thick collar of diamonds set in platinum mail. She employed the best masseuse and physio-culturist in Europe, so that her breasts pushed out fiercely from beneath her white silk shirt (cut by Dior), culminating in hard, menacing points, like the tips of Howitzers poking out from pill-boxes. Her matador trousers were royal purple satin, revealing every curve and ripple of her thighs and beyond, with pearls set in a mesh of thin gold wire running down the seams. Even her gold satin pumps were set with pearls. She must have been about forty-five.

'Please don't get up'. She held out to Henry a hard, brown hand, with silver-painted fingernails. 'You brought my little essay, Mr.——?'

'Arnold—Henry Arnold.'

'You have pretty hair, Mr. Arnold. Did anyone ever tell you that?'

'I don't—think so'. said Henry, pulling the article from his pocket. He felt like a young Russian guardsman talking to the Empress Catherine.

'Don't kid me, young man. O.K.—hand it over.'

She sat down on a nearby sofa, tucked her feet under her, pushed her dark glasses up over her forehead, and began to read.

'It got a bit messy, so I had it typed out again', said Henry nervously.

'So I see', said she, continuing to read. 'I got a teeny bit angry with the young man whose place you've taken. Perhaps you heard about it? He tried to horn in on my political opinions. Some sort of Socialist, I guess. Now you wouldn't try to do that, would you, Mr. Arnold?'

'Of course not. I did, however, make a few alterations in the er—style.'

'Sure. I know I can't write elegant English. But I have a sharp eye for a slant I didn't put in. Help yourself to a drink—in the commode over there.'

Henry walked over to an exquisite Boule cabinet and opened the doors. A huge tray of glasses and bottles sprang out at him on a spring. His hand shaking, he poured a few drops of whisky into a heavy, cut-glass tumbler. He sipped the drink in silence while Madame Plympton continued to read. Ten minutes passed. Finally, she put down the papers and readjusted her glasses.

'Mr. Arnold, you have a genuine talent. You've got my message across powerfully. I could use you here. What do they pay you at *France-Miracle?*'

'As a matter of fact, I'm not quite sure.'

'Not *sure?*'

'Well, I've only just joined them you see. The question of my salary has not been—fully discussed, as yet.'

'Mr. Arnold, money is the one thing you should *always* be sure about. Anyway, whatever it is, I'll double it. How does that proposition strike you?'

'That's extremely generous of you, madame, but I don't quite see how——'

'Don't be worried that I'll make a pass at you. You're not my type.'

'Believe me, such a thing never occurred to me. It's just that, I only started two days ago, and it would seem rather disloyal——'

'O.K., O.K., I respect your finer feelings. Do you smoke?'

'Occasionally.'

She opened a drawer of the low table which lay at the foot of the sofa, and pulled out a gold cigarette case.

'Catch'. She threw the cigarette case into Henry's lap. 'It's by Cartier. Keep it.'

Henry picked up the glittering object, long and slim, with a pattern of wild roses etched in black enamel. 'But madame, I couldn't possibly keep it—it must be worth a great deal of money.'

'Sure. It is. I'm a rich woman, Mr. Arnold, and when somebody does something that pleases me, I like to give 'em something in return. Otherwise, what's the point in being rich? So don't say another word. Keep it. Or sell it if you want. I don't mind. And now I'm going to keep you waiting just a few more minutes, while one of my secretaries types out a couple of new paragraphs to add on to this. Something that darling Monsieur Pleven told me at dinner last night. Wait here, and she'll bring it down'. She stepped into the lift. 'And you must come to one of my parties soon.' The panel slid back, and Henry was left holding the cigarette case.

He was deeply perplexed. Faced with the alternative of returning to London a failure, he had accepted the job at *France-Miracle* without really bothering to think what it entailed; and since he had begun work, so many things seemed to have happened that he had still not considered the ethics of his position. Madame Plympton's blatant, almost brutal gesture brought him back to reality. She had given him a present, worth at least £100, for successfully 'ghosting' a politically criminal article, not one word of which he believed to be true. Henry did not know very much about French politics, but he was quite sure that the Algerian war was entirely wicked; and the only purpose of Madame Plympton's article was to convince gullible, high-placed Americans that it was a just cause. Moreover, by re-writing it, he had helped to make it more convincing. Could anything be more reprehensible? Henry absent-mindedly took a sip of his whisky; then realized what he was doing, and set the tumbler firmly on the table. He could not possibly partake of Madame Plympton's hospitality, even in the smallest degree. For all he knew, the whisky was financed by Algerian oil shares (it was not; Madame Plympton was much too shrewd a business-woman to invest in such speculative commodities). And he would simply leave the cigarette case on the table.

But what of his position at *France-Miracle?* Wasn't this exactly the same thing—only not quite so obvious? The paper was confessedly a French propaganda sheet, financed from secret funds. By working for it, he was not merely sharing in the guilt of the French government, he was actively aiding it. He was a paid hack, a hired political assassin. But if he left, it was highly unlikely he would find another job. He would therefore have to return to London. This was unthinkable. The only possible way in which he could reconcile remaining at *France-Miracle* with his conscience was by accepting Edgar's suggestion—and sabotaging it. But how? And anyway, didn't this raise another problem of conscience? Henry was beginning to realize that living in Paris was a permanent conflict between morality and expediency. (This is a truism, and applies anywhere, but in Paris so many truisms seem new.)

Henry's train of thought was rudely broken by two hands thrust across his eyes, and a voice which said: 'Guess who?' It was female, and unmistakable. And yet it seemed incredible.

'Cleo', he said, twisting round. The hands were withdrawn.

136

'Good boy. How clever of you to guess, considering we've only met once.' She was radiant in a high-necked primrose cotton dress. 'Here's the article.'

'Good lord', said Henry, 'do you work here?'

'Didn't you know? I live here. The old painted doll is my stepmother.'

'So you're not one of her secretaries?'

'Heavens, no. I was upstairs and heard a young man from *France-Miracle* was around. I guessed it would be you, and offered to bring the thing down. What do you think of her?'

'Well——' began Henry.

'I know—she's ghastly. She's made Papa ghastly too. He married her after my mother died, when I was twelve. My mother was English, you know. In those days, Papa was just a nice, cheerful old voluptuary, who spent his time between here and Cannes, chasing girls. Then he married her for her money, and since then he's become a sort of power-mad politician, mixed up with all sorts of terrible people. They spend hours here, plotting. My stepmother eggs him on. I hate them both.'

'Cleo, you shouldn't say such things about your parents.'

'Oh, don't be such a bloody prig. You've got no idea what they're like.' Her voice was high-pitched, shrill almost. For an instant, Henry saw what it must mean to live in this house, loaded with wealth and vulgarity and—corruption, he supposed.

'I'm sorry, Cleo. That was a silly thing to say.'

'It's all right. I must go now. Paul will show you out.' She turned to walk from the room. There was something cold and sad about her figure, despite its gay dress. Henry rose.

'Cleo?'

'Yes?'

'Could you—would you like to meet me for a drink sometime?'

Cleo turned round slowly. 'I was hoping you'd ask me that. When?'

Something inside Henry gave a great leap of joy. 'Anytime. Whenever you like.'

'This evening, then. At the Deux Magots. Six-thirty. Good-bye.' She opened the massive double doors of the salon, and was gone. He could hear her footsteps tapping up the marble staircase. The butler showed him to the front door, but when he opened it a great gust of rain blew in: an April shower had begun to fall while Henry was immured in the great, overheated house. Without a word, the butler produced a huge umbrella, of the type used by commissionaires, and escorted Henry to the gates. The idea, presumably, was to escort Henry to his car. But since he had no car, the butler about-turned at the gates, and marched back with the umbrella into the house, leaving Henry in the rain. It took him ten minutes to find a taxi, and it was only after he had clambered into it, and was driving back to the office, that he discovered the cigarette case nestling in his pocket. In one second his doubts were resolved: he would sell it, and use the proceeds for taking out Cleo.

It was still raining when he entered the Deux Magots, just before six-thirty that evening. The red-plush seats were crowded, the waiters busy serving hot *tisanes* to damp figures in duffle coats and mackintoshes. Henry looked round anxiously, but there was, fortunately, no-one he knew there; a meeting with Dora, say, would have been awkward. He sat down, ordered a *fine à l'eau* and took out a copy of *Le Monde* which had been screwed up in his pocket. '*Le Ministère Gaillard de Nouveau Menacé*' ran the headline. After nearly a month of calm, Jacques Fauvet informed his readers, the general debate on government policy, scheduled for next week, presented perilous pitfalls for M. Felix Gaillard and his colleagues. It was rumoured in the *couloirs* of the Palais Bourbon that M. Jacques Soustelle intended to make a full-scale assault on the government in an effort to bring it down and replace it with a government of national safety. The Socialists and M.R.P. were determined to support the government, the Radicals were divided, a large block of the Moderates would refuse their confidence. . . . The cabinet had sat for five hours that morning. . . .

'Can I have a little of your attention, please?' She was already sitting opposite him, hatless, drops of rain glistening on her dark hair and on her fur coat—mink he guessed—which she wore pulled loosely round her body. She held out her hand to him.

'Feel that.'

'Freezing, you poor thing.'

'Yes. Buy me a cognac and hot water, please.'

He summoned the waiter. Then, somewhat at a loss what to say next, he remarked: 'The news is very serious.'

'Yes. The ministry will fall next week. Then they will try and overthrow the régime and set up a Fascist dictatorship. They're up at my father's house now—Soustelle and all the rest. Locked in the library on the long-distance telephone to Algiers.'

'Is it really as serious as all that?'

'Of course it is. Papa phones Algiers almost every day, and talks to one of the generals at army headquarters.

He's called Massu—I've met him, a vulgar little man with a big nose, rather like that horrid Zarpeg, really. He commands the parachute troops in Algiers. If they don't get their way in the Assembly, they'll simply take over by force. And then they'll start killing people here as well as in Algeria. I hate them.'

'But if your father's mixed up with them, why do you stay at home? Why don't you get a job and move out? You could model or something.'

'Because, if I stay at home, I hear what they're up to. I'm more useful to the Party that way.'

'The Party? You mean the *Communist* Party?'

'Of course. Look.' She opened her handbag and pulled out a small folded piece of cardboard. It read: *Parti Communiste Français. Paris: Sous-section du Seizième Arrondissement. Candidat-Membre Numéro 4561. Cléo-Marie La Fouette.* 'I only joined a few weeks ago, so I'm still a candidate member.'

'But this is fantastic, Cleo.' Henry's sensible, liberal conscience—as well as perhaps deeper feelings—was outraged that this beautiful, intelligent, highly individualist girl should be a Communist. 'How can you be a Communist after Hungary and all that? Surely there must be a better way of combating these people?'

'No. The Socialists? They sold out two years ago over Algeria. Mollet is a sort of Fascist, he's only interested in being boss of the party machine. He'll help the *colons*—you'll see.'

'But what about Mendès-France?' For a long time, Henry had been told that Mendès-France was the only 'good' French politician.

'Yes—but he has no party, no organization. Only the Communists are capable of putting up a fight. You see,

I'm not interested in theory. I care about Algerians being tortured and murdered, and I care about France. Don't you understand—there's nothing that people like myself can do except join in with the Communists.' She looked at her watch. 'As a matter of fact, I'm waiting for my party contact now. I have to tell him what went on at the house to-day.'

'Oh' said Henry. He was bitterly disappointed. She had merely arranged to meet him as a cover for seeing somebody else.

'I know what you're thinking', said Cleo. 'And it's wrong. I'm not using you as a stool-pigeon.' She smiled at him—a warm, young girl's smile—and squeezed his hand. 'I only heard what was going on after you left, and telephoned my contact to meet me here. You don't mind, do you? Look, here he comes.'

It was Henry's rescuer, Pierre-Emile. With him was a much older man, with close-cropped, greying hair. They both carried umbrellas.

'Cleo, *chérie*', said Pierre-Emile, in an easy, familiar way which sent a sharp shaft through Henry's heart. Was he her lover? Would that explain her conversion to Communism? 'And my English friend, too!' He smiled at Henry, but the glance he shot at Cleo was questioning.

'He's all right', said Cleo. 'He won't talk.'

'Good. Then let me present Monsieur Arpad, of the Bureau.' They all shook hands and sat down. Henry gathered that Arpad was a party official. He was a sharp-faced, taciturn man, who merely grunted from time to time, nodding his head, and sipping black coffee in quick, nervous motions.

Cleo told them of the gathering at her father's house, late that afternoon. She gave the names of those present, and Henry, watching Arpad's face, could see he was memorizing them.

'I listened from outside the door of the library', said Cleo. 'I didn't hear everything, but I gathered that as soon as they get rid of Gaillard, their tactics will be to prevent anyone from forming a government, and allow pressure to build up in Algiers.'

'But can they overthrow Gaillard?' asked Pierre-Emile.

'One of them said he was sure of only two hundred and forty votes.'

'Nine-five Socialists, seventy M.R.P. . . .'

'Twenty-three Radicals will vote with him.'

'And the Independents d'Outre-Mer. That makes two hundred and seven.'

'He's sure of about forty Independents.'

'What will Pinay do? Abstain?'

'No. Vote against. He's told them. And Bidault, too.'

'How many M.R.P. votes can Bidault swing? Ten?'

'Less. Only five. But Mendès will vote against. That makes twelve more. And Mitterrand and six of the U.D.S.R., and five *non-inscrit*.'

'Forty-five Poujadistes. Thirty Radicals, at least. Forty Independents and Peasants.'

'That makes one hundred and sixty, probably more. It all depends on the C.P.'

'The party', said Arpad, speaking for the first time, 'will naturally vote against.'

'Then the government will fall. You must be mad. Do you want to let in the Fascists?'

'Impossible. The only way they could do it would be through De Gaulle. And Washington would not dare

142

risk De Gaulle. It might mean a *renversement des alliances*. Your alarm is premature, my friend.'

'But if Gaillard falls, the centre coalition can't be reconstructed. What will happen?'

'The *ouverture à gauche*, comrade,' said Arpad. 'Mitterrand will form a left-centre government, with the party's support. It is the only answer to the equation.'

'Washington would be even more opposed to that. And I don't believe Coty would ever call Mitterrand.'

'This discussion is pointless, comrade', said Arpad, rising to go. 'Thank you for your information, *Mademoiselle*. I will see it is conveyed to quarters where it may prove useful.' He bowed unsmilingly and left.

'He's a fool', said Cleo fiercely. 'The party are going to do just what my father wants them to do.'

'Perhaps. But the party knows best. It *must* know best.'

'Rubbish', said Henry, energetically. 'They just think in terms of Soviet foreign policy. For all you know, Moscow would *like* De Gaulle to be in power.'

'I can't believe it', said Pierre-Emile. 'If it's true, democracy in France will be lost. I shall emigrate to Canada.'

'And I shall go to England', said Cleo. 'Will you take me to England, Henry?'

Her tone of voice was flippant, but Henry blushed deeply nonetheless. 'Naturally', he said, attempting to be equally flippant, and failing miserably. Pierre-Emile grinned.

'I see you've made a conquest, Cleo. Well, I must leave you two turtle-doves and get back to work. Phone me if you hear anything else, Cleo'.

'I'm sorry about this', said Cleo to Henry when Pierre-Emile had gone. 'But there wasn't any other time when

I could meet them. And I shall have to fly back in a minute—they're expecting me at dinner. Can I have another drink? I'll need it if I have to face that crowd.'

'Of course', said Henry, and signalled to the waiter. When it came, Cleo gulped it down and then took Henry's hand.

'Do you like me, Henry?'

'Yes.'

'A lot?' He nodded.

'Then do something for me. Help me with this—this business.'

'But how can I help?'

'In lots of ways. Things are coming to a crisis. I may have to leave home. Promise?'

'All right. And will you tell me something in return? You're not in love with Pierre-Emile, are you?'

'Heavens, no. What an extraordinary idea. I've known him since we were children. He has a girl friend who works for Mainbocher.'

'He didn't convert you to Communism?'

'Of course not. And I'm not a convert: I don't believe in Communism. I just felt I had to do something, so I went straight along to their headquarters and plonked my money down. They were very suspicious at first. They still are. You saw the way that rather sinister little man behaved.'

'But Cleo, it seems so absurd that a beautiful young girl like you should be a Communist.'

'Why shouldn't I be, if I want to? I suppose you think women haven't got minds. Perhaps you are a prig after all. I can see we wouldn't get on. I'll find somebody else to take me to England. Or, for that matter, I'll go myself.'

'Please, Cleo—you know I didn't mean to sound patronising.'

'Of course. I was only joking. And now I must dash. You look very dependable, really.' She leaned over and kissed him lightly on the cheek. 'Don't phone me at home. I'll ring you at your office. By the way, what's your home address?'

'The Paris-Palace.'

'Horrors! All right, I'll remember it. Good-bye.'

'Good-bye.' It was only after she had passed through the swing doors that Henry noticed she had left a 10,000 franc note for him to pay the bill.

This set up a distressing train of thought in Henry's mind. In its almost insultingly casual way, the banknote reminded him that he was a penniless young man, with no achievements, and no particular talents, and that Cleo was the beautiful daughter of a millionaire. As has been said before, Henry did not bother very much about money—he had never had to—still less about class. He came from the bourgeoisie and he had always implicitly assumed he would spend his life among the bourgeoisie, on the assumption of course that there is a money-grubbing bourgeoisie and an art-making one, and that his affinities would be with the latter.

Meeting Cleo introduced not merely a new person, but a new element into his life. For the first time, Henry took a hard look at his current and future prospects. It was not enough now merely to see Cleo again—however unlikely that had seemed only the day before. He now wanted her, permanently and for his own. And it was only when he admitted this fact to himself—as he did now, sitting at the café table and gazing at the note—that he realized the absolute hopelessness of his position. He had nothing to offer Cleo beyond the fact that he was sane, healthy, reasonably presentable and (he thought) above average intelligence. Obviously, every odiously wealthy, smart and titled young man in Europe already was, or soon would be, pursuing her. She claimed to be a radical. Superficially, at any rate, she might think she despised such things as money, power or position. But she was very young—perhaps only twenty—and the phase would not last long. Her parents, who were certainly worldly and probably unscrupulous, would make sure that she was prevented from making any rash move until she had learnt their schemes of values. For the first time in his life, Henry wanted money and fame—not in the dreamy, abstract way in which a young man longs for them, but with the hard, urgent appetite of a starving man craving food.

Acquiring fame was a slow business. But money? It was sometimes made overnight. All one needed was capital. Henry fingered the slim cigarette case in his pocket.

Edgar the poet, who usually prowled the boulevard cafés at this time of evening, slid into the chair opposite him.

'Well, and how go your efforts for the Quai d'Orsay? I heard you got the job.'

'Yes. I'm very, very grateful to you. Have a drink.'

'Thanks—a Beaujolais, if I may. You look exceedingly gloomy. Have you lost more money, or simply more virtue?'

'No. I'm in love.'

Edgar laughed, flashing his sharp teeth. 'My good Henry, the devastating obviousness with which you descend into Parisian life is quite breathtaking. You'll be glad to hear I'm writing a little poem about you, which begins,

> Whither go'est thou, pin-striped youth
> On the boulevard wild,
> With bowler lost, and tie uncouth,
> With what dread drug beguiled?

"Dread drug" is rather good, don't you think? And who is the woman who has supplanted Dora in your affections?'

'Don't compare her to that bitch', said Henry fiercely.

'A thousand pardons. But that reminds me of another verse—

> It was a *garçonne* slim and sad
> Who stole away my heart.
> For in between her thighs she had
> The key to Modern Art.

She *is* French I take it?'

'Half French, half English. Her father is a ruffianly right-wing deputy, her stepmother an American millionairess.'

'Oh, but my dear boy, I *know* about her. Cleo la Fouette, much photographed at Cannes, St. Moritz and other upper-crust honey pots, surrounded by Aly Khans and various rich darkies. Since said to have read a book and gone serious.'

'She's a Communist.'

'But of course. Always from one extreme to another. A Leonora Fini or a Tâchiste. An Ella Wheeler Wilcox or a Kathleen Raine. Women never vary. However, how nice to have an heiress in the party! How the comrades will rub their calloused hands! And this, no doubt, has accelerated the process of your own conversion. Shall I lend you my signed copy of the *Manifesto?*'

'No. Tell me how I can make a lot of money quickly.'

'Ask Dora. She raised 150,000 francs overnight to get the unworthy Crick out of jug. I can't think how. You might, of course, finance a new poetry review I am thinking of giving birth to—but the financial returns may be slow in accruing.'

'No.'

'Or put your available cash on a horse. But then *have* you any cash?'

'I've got this.' Henry produced the cigarette case. 'I could sell it.'

'Have you got a receipt? No? Then it would be rather tricky in this suspicious city. I'll tell you what: I know a little man, in a little shop, in a little street, not so very far away, who'd probably be willing to oblige. You give me ten per cent of the lolly, and I'll take it round now.'

'O.K.' Henry handed it over, and Edgar sidled off on his errand.

He came back triumphantly twenty minutes later, and handed Henry 100,000 francs in crisp, 10,000 franc notes.

'Ten thousand I keep', he said. 'Bliss. I think, to be realistic, we were rather done. Your very vulgar case was probably worth 200,000, to judge by the ease with which the bargain was concluded.'

'Thanks', said Henry, pocketing the money. 'Tell me something, Edgar. Why do you do these things for me?'

'*Not* disinterested affection. I act as the devil's advocate to you, making it possible for you to descend still

further into the pit. I look forward to the total dis-
integration of your bourgeois personality. And now I
must be off to tempt others.'

'Stop. Before you go—tell me the name of a horse.'

'*Petit-Salaud*, running in the 3.00 at Auteuil tomorrow.
I overheard a surrealist painter recommend it in a bar.'

There was no *Petit Salaud* running at Auteuil the next
day, as Henry discovered when he opened his morning
paper. The nearest approach was *Salade de Laitu* in the
3.30 at Longchamps. At lunchtime, after asking Francie's
advice, he put the 100,000 francs on it at a Pari-Mutuel
office. It won, at five to one, long odds for France. He
now had 500,000 francs and, after office hours, split
a bottle of Champagne with the two girls.

'Tell me', he asked Francie, as she was leaving to
catch her bus, 'what do you think of Cleo?'

'Oh dear', said Francie. 'You've fallen for her. It was
bound to happen, I suppose, but Regina and I liked you
so much and we were getting so used to you. Now you'll
leave.'

'What do you mean?'

'Well, either you'll run off with her or—far more
likely—La Plympton will get to hear about it and
Rupert will get a chilly little note from Taxim telling
him you're fired.'

Madame Plympton, however, remained in ignorance
of his passion for Cleo, at least so far as Henry knew.
But on Monday, a chilly little note did arrive from
M. Taxim. Half-way through the morning, Sir Rupert
came out of his office and surveyed the two girls and
Henry majestically.

'The credulity and inaccuracy of the French', he

said, 'continues to astonish me, though I have lived among them for nearly fifteen years. After a decade of service, my valet is still convinced that all Englishmen dislike ice in their whisky and invariably fails to provide me with an adequate supply for the evening. My *concierge* is determined to sell me her daughter and dresses her up in black stockings in the fond belief that this will whet my appetite. I believe they got all this nonsense from *Les Carnets de Major Thompson* or some such foolish book. Another popular delusion here is that Englishmen are always plotting to undermine the French. *L'Albion perfide* and so on. Taxim, as I have learnt from past experience, is peculiarly vulnerable to these hallucinations. I received a letter from him this morning, informing me that a member of my staff, one Henry Arnold, is a British Secret Service Agent. He claims that he has received anonymous but circumstantial information to this effect.'

There was consternation in the room. Francie and Regina looked at each other. Henry looked down at his desk. Sir Rupert, ignoring them, continued.

'I have replied to his letter, informing him that, not only do I not employ a member of the British Secret Service on my staff, but equally and perhaps more to the point, that I do not employ anyone called Henry Arnold. You, Charles, I take it, are not a Secret Service Agent?'

'No', said Henry.

'Of course not. Most disagreeable people. Invariably dirty and usually ineffectual. I had painful dealings with them during the war.'

He returned to his office and shut the door. Regina looked solemn, but Francie burst into laughter.

'From now on, we'll *all* have to call you Charles. *Are* you, by the way, a British agent?'

'No', said Henry angrily. 'And I wish to hell I knew who said I was.'

Afterwards, he remembered: Crick. He was the only person in Paris who disliked him enough to go to the trouble of finding out who kept an eye on *France-Miracle* in the Quai d'Orsay, and to write an anonymous letter to him. He might have written to other people, too: the police, for instance. Henry knew enough about France to know that foreigners were not allowed to accept jobs without a *carte de travail*. Sir Rupert had so far said nothing about procuring him one, and in any case was far too detached to descend to such minor details. The police would probably not believe that he was a secret agent; but they might well make enquiries and ask to see his papers. Then his illegal existence would come out. Crick might by now, moreover, have discovered the name of his hotel, and started making trouble there. There seemed no way of placating him, short of offering him money, and this Henry was unwilling to do at any cost; the memory of the £80 still rankled. It was all very worrying.

Even more worrying, as the week progressed, was the silence of Cleo. The depressing history of Henry's previous relations with women—especially those with any pretensions to beauty—inclined him to believe that she had simply forgotten him, her refusal to allow him to telephone her being a simple device to avoid the embarrassment of refusing his invitations. But this hardly squared with her attitude, which had been spontaneously friendly, inviting even. Perhaps her father had got wind of her Communist activities and had locked her up somewhere in the country. From what Henry had heard, he would certainly be capable of it. If so, should Henry go to her rescue? And how should he set about it? She might well be under twenty-one, the legal age of consent. If Henry interfered, this could provide the Count with an excuse for getting him expelled from France—he was the sort of man who would have powerful friends in the Ministry of the Interior. Henry decided to lie low for a few more days, and then make discreet enquiries about Cleo's whereabouts.

Meanwhile, the routine of *France-Miracle* went on. There was no further word from Taxim about Henry's alleged activities, though he must have been mystified by Sir Rupert's letter, since Henry's name was by now officially registered on the firm's payroll. Francie and Henry, with occasional assistance from Regina, put together the current issue of the magazine, sticking up the articles on big sheets of white paper, and then taking them to the printers on the far side of Montparnasse. There was a last minute panic, just before press day, when it was discovered that an entire article was missing. Eventually, Francie discovered that Sir Rupert had taken it home, proofs, dummy and all, in order to do what he called 'a spot of editing'. It was retrieved from his flat—a soggy mess of paper smeared with a red, sticky substance.

'Jam', said Sir Rupert, when asked for an explanation by Francie. 'Ordinary strawberry jam. I thought I'd better stick it up, to save time you know, and found I hadn't any paste at home. So I used jam. It seems to have worked very well.'

Sir Rupert continued to call Henry Charles, but obviously regarded him with affection. They drank a lot of tea together in the café across the street and occasionally lunched at a restaurant near Les Invalides. April was now in full blossom, the weather cold, but fine and sunny, and Sir Rupert liked to have his meals outdoors, sitting on the restaurant's terrace.

'I knew you'd be a success at this job', he said to Henry one day. 'People think a magazine is a complicated thing. It isn't. Running one is the easiest thing in the world. That's why I leave it all to Francie. You and I, my boy, need time to reflect on *policy*. Can't be caught up in all the tiny details.'

'No.'

'Taxim's always fussing, of course. Typical of a Frenchman. D'you like the French?'

'Not much.'

'Neither do I. Hate 'em. I just like the way they live, that's all. Only reason why I'm here. Of course, they're going down hill rapidly. A big bust-up's due soon, revolution and all that, you know. The government's due to fall this week, and then it'll start.'

'But it was due to fall last week.'

'I know. It's always the same. Every week they say there's going to be a crisis, and just when one's getting bored with the thing, there *is*. I've lived through fourteen here. I hear Madame Plympton's husband is planning something fishy. By the way, how do you get on with her?'

'I've only met her once. She gave me a gold cigarette case.'

'From Cartier, I trust?'

'Yes.'

'That's right: insist on nothing less than the best. She once offered me £50,000 a year if I'd marry her. Before she met the Count, of course. I said I'd take nothing less than £100,000. A Fitzhoward, I told her, always sells his life dearly. She didn't think it was funny and ended the negotiations. Pity—I could have done with the money.'

'Her stepdaughter is very beautiful.'

'Cleo? Yes: I suppose so. Too young for me. Only nineteen, you know. I'm afraid I like jaded creatures in their mid-thirties. Then you don't get all that girlish chatter and tears before bedtime. Give me a plump Jewess of thirty-five, preferably married. They're always affectionate, obedient and discreet. And of course there's no nonsense about divorcing their husbands and marrying you. But you'd better watch your step with Cleo.'

'Why?'

'She's a man-eater, my boy. She'll swallow you alive. I've known her since she was a little girl. Before you know where you are, you'll be involved in some mad scheme of hers and get into endless trouble. Then, when she's finished with you, she'll drop you flat. She's very tough, Charles—much too tough for you.'

'I'm afraid I'm already a little involved with her.'

'Then get disinvolved, fast. That's an order, Charles. I can't afford to lose you in the office.'

That night, a Tuesday, the government fell. 'The crisis', declared *Le Figaro* the next morning, 'is not a routine one: it is the crisis of our institutions, the crisis of the Republic.' Paris, nonetheless, was taking it calmly. There were no demonstrations, no extra policemen. Henry walked to his office along the Quai, in perfect spring weather. Pale golden sunshine lit the dark barrier of the Louvre across the Seine and the white arches of the bridges. At the open-air swimming pool in the river, workmen were repainting the woodwork, ready for the summer season. There were flower-sellers outside the Quai d'Orsay, which looked sleepy and subdued. The guards outside the National Assembly yawned and scratched themselves. Two or three bored reporters hung around the gates, waiting for the first arrivals.

Half way through the morning, a messenger boy came to the office with a letter for Henry. Inside was a huge, embossed invitation-card. La Comtesse Honor Plympton-La Fouette requests the pleasure of Mr Henry Arnold's company at an evening reception on Friday, 18 April, at 9 p.m. *Cravats Noirs*. On the back was scrawled: 'You must come. Have had terrible troubles and want to talk to you. Cleo.' Henry hurriedly wrote out an acceptance, addressed it to Madame Plympton, and handed it to the messenger. He desperately wanted to write a note to Cleo also, but decided the risk was too great: it might fall into her stepmother's hands.

The next three days were an intolerable period of waiting. Cleo was obviously having difficulties with her parents. But a reception was scarcely the best opportunity for a private talk. Why hadn't Cleo telephoned, as arranged? Henry had other grounds for uneasiness. On Wednesday evening, when he returned to his hotel, Madame Marcourt reported that a stranger had called and made enquiries about him; from her description, he was obviously a plain-clothes detective. This might be for any one of three reasons—the affair of the policeman beaten up by Pierre-Emile and his friend, the fight in the Rhumerie de Guadeloupe, or the spy-mania of Taxim. Madame, too, evidently believed the caller was a policeman: her attitude to Henry became distinctly chilly. Henry, reflecting on his already lengthy record of crime, had an instinctive feeling that his days in Paris were drawing to a close, and that the future of Henry Arnold, as well as the Republic, was at stake.

On Friday evening, Henry dined early, arrayed himself in his dinner jacket which he retrieved, somewhat crumpled, from the bottom of his still-packed suitcase, and took a taxi to Passy. It was close on ten o'clock when he arrived at the house, and the road outside was already double-parked with limousines. Groups of chauffeurs hung around, smoking, and there were a good many policemen. As before, Henry was escorted to the house and handed over to the butler, who took his coat. The hall was crowded with people, spilling over from the two vast salons which opened out on either side of it. Madame Plympton was nowhere to be seen.

Henry edged his way unobtrusively into the Blue Salon. Most of the furniture had been taken away, and the room now held a hundred or more guests. Along one of the walls, tables, covered with white and gold silk tablecloths, were laid with food: salmon, caviare, lobster, roast hams and turkeys, wild-boar, sucking pig, cold venison and duck and every conceivable kind of *charcutérie*. Behind the tables stood a dozen waiters, dispensing Champagne. Henry knew nobody present, though he recognized a number of well-known political faces, a famous film-star, two best-selling novelists and the winner of last year's Tour de France. Evidently, *le tout Paris* was here. But where was Cleo? Henry took a glass of Champagne and sipped it nervously. There was a sudden influx of new guests, and the room became uncomfortably crowded. He found himself wedged between the arm of a sofa and a Chinese lacquer cabinet crowded with jade; behind him, Van Gogh's self-portrait breathed down the back of his neck. Three plump men, each with the rosette of the Legion d'Honneur, hemmed him in, talking rapidly.

'Pleven should never have been designated.'

'That is correct. He is obstinate, like all Bretons. He has no chance, but he will waste time with futile consultations.'

'He telephoned me this morning and offered me Agriculture.'

'He offered me the Interior. I told him not to be a fool.'

'I said I'd accept if the Socialists came in.'

'Impossible. Mollet is waiting for the crisis to mature.'

'There are only three choices: Bidault, Mitterrand, or—De Gaulle.'

'Bonn will back Bidault.'

'Moscow will back De Gaulle.'

'The Americans will back Pflimlin.'

'So will I.'

'And I.'

'Right. You turn down Bidault, I'll turn down Mitterrand.'

'*D'accord.*'

'Then, if Pflimlin offers me Finance, I'll accept on condition you go to the Interior.'

'Yes, provided a Radical goes to the Quai d'Orsay.'

'But that means a Catholic at the Rue St. Dominique. It is unprecedented since Dreyfus.'

'Alternatively, a Moderate at Education, provided he is *laïc.*'

'They can keep Industry.'

'And the Colonies. That should satisfy them. Then we take Education also?'

'Yes. But who goes to Algiers?'

'Exactly, my friend. Algiers is the key. If we prolong the crisis another three weeks or, better still, four, we get Pflimlin and reconstruct the centre coalition. It is logically inevitable. But, meanwhile, what happens in Algiers?'

'That reminds me—where is Soustelle? Is he here?'

'Yes, with Fouette in the library.'

'They are in contact with Algiers?'

'Fouette has installed a new telephone exchange here. It is no longer possible for us to tap his line.'

'We must watch him. He has at least three prefects eating out of his hand.'

'And the inspector-generals of the gendarmerie.'

'When I go to the Interior I shall place him under house-arrest.'

'Be careful. This room is too full. Shall we have more Champagne?'

'Excellent. A good crisis always makes me thirsty.'

The three men shuffled off, waddling fat behinds. Henry, released, struggled slowly towards the door, looking for Cleo. There was a sudden stir, a falling-back of the crowd, and Jacques Soustelle, accompanied by Madame Plympton and a stocky, dark-haired man whom Henry realized was the Count, walked into the room. As the political assassin of Felix Gaillard, and an unknown force for the future, Soustelle was the man of the moment. The noise of conversation fell several decibels: all eyes were turned on the trio, as they moved towards the bar. An elderly, white-haired gentleman, wearing full evening dress and the Grand Cross of the Legion d'Honneur, stepped out of the crowd and seized Soustelle by the hand.

'You must save the honour of France', he said.

'Count on me', said Soustelle, drily, turning towards the bar.

At the other end of the room, a voice shouted: '*Vive Soustelle*', and another, '*Vive De Gaulle*'. There was a perceptible moment of tension, then a young woman standing near Henry giggled, and people began to talk again.

' . . . now we know France will stand firm in Algeria.'

'We shall get rid of the old gang at the Palais Bourbon . . .'

'And the Jews . . .'

' . . . outlaw the Communist Party.'

'The workers will have to watch out.'

'A wage-freeze.'

'No more arms for Bourguiba.'

' . . . smash Nasser.'

' . . . tell the Americans where they get off . . .'

' . . . and the British.'

'The Russians only respect a strong man and a strong government.'

'So do the Arabs . . .'

' . . . no more scuttles.'

' . . . no more negotiations.'

'De Gaulle will cut the subsidies . . .'

'Suppress *Le Monde* . . .'

' . . . and *L'Express*.'

'Arrest the defeatists . . .'

'*Les fossoyeurs* . . .'

'*Les architectes des abandons* . . .'

'We must make our own H-bombs.'

'And reopen the brothels.'

'The Army's with us.'

'The Church, too . . .'

'The police . . . the gendarmerie . . . the gardes mobiles . . .'

'Henry!' an urgent voice whispered in his ear. 'Thank goodness I've found you.' Cleo was wearing an oyster-coloured satin dress, knee-length, with a spray of diamond flowers hanging from a gold chain round her neck.

'I couldn't get out of this room,' said Henry. 'I was trapped by three fat politicians engaged in cabinet building. Why didn't you get in touch with me before?'

'I've been away. I'll explain everything as soon as we can talk together properly. I daren't use the telephone here any more. Papa's had a new system installed, and all the extensions go through a switchboard.'

'Good God!'

'Look. I'm going to make my way back to my room. Join me there in a few minutes. It's on the first floor. Turn right at the top of the staircase, and it's the last room on the left. If you run into anyone, pretend you're looking for the loo or something. Is that clear?'

'Yes.'

She slipped away through the crowd, and Henry saw her whisper something to her stepmother. Then she left the room. Henry hovered near the bar, drank another glass of Champagne, then slipped unobtrusively into the hall. He walked slowly up the wide staircase, pretending to study a large bacchanalia by Rubens which hung on the wall.

'Excuse me sir, can I help you?' A footman—or rather somebody dressed as a footman—barred his way at the top of the stairs.

'Yes. I'm looking for the lavatory.'

'Certainly, sir. Follow me, sir.' The footman led him back down the stairs, along a corridor, and into a cloakroom. Henry, sweating slightly, waited two or three minutes in the cloakroom, then returned to the hall, mingling in the crowd at the foot of the stairs. The footman was back in position again. How on earth could he get past him? Why hadn't Cleo thought of this? He remembered Sir Rupert's words—'Before you know where you are, you'll be involved in some mad scheme of hers and get into endless trouble.' This was undoubtedly true. He had scarcely had a tranquil thought since he had met her. Even if he got upstairs, how would he get down again? The footman, or detective, had clearly been placed there for some purpose. Henry saw himself being apprehended somewhere on the first floor, charged with intent to steal some of the valuable objects with which the house seemed to be overloaded, and handed over to the police. The obvious and sensible thing would be simply to walk out of the house and never give Cleo another thought: he had enough troubles already. But Henry, though shy, was not a coward. He was also, and firmly, in love. He was determined to get up the stairs at all costs.

A sudden commotion in the hall gave him his opportunity. One of the three portly politicians slipped on the polished parquet floor, collided heavily with a woman in a backless evening dress, and fell on his back. The woman screamed—iced Champagne was trickling down her vertebrae—and the footman darted down the stairs to restore order. Whilst he was helping the injured senator to his feet, Henry quickly gained the landing, and vanished out of sight behind a massive Louis Quatorze court-cupboard. So far as he knew, nobody had seen him.

F

He ran down the corridor and tapped lightly on the door at the end. It opened immediately.

'What an age you've been', said Cleo, locking the door behind him.

'There's a flunkey barring the top of the stairs.'

'*Merde!* It can't be to guard the guests' furs—they're downstairs. This house is getting like a prison. Well, anyway, I'll get you out somehow. Come and sit down.'

Cleo's room was large, with a balcony looking out over the street. It was furnished in what the French call *le style anglais*—rosewood Regency upholstered in yellow satin. There was a vast four-poster bed, a desk, a chaise-longue, and a huge Regency sofa, with modern spring upholstery. The walls were entirely covered with bookcases.

Henry sat down on the sofa. From a tiny refrigerator let into a cabinet by the side of the bed, Cleo produced a bottle of Champagne. She opened it with what seemed to Henry considerable professional skill, and handed him a glass.

'Thanks. Cleo, is it true you're only nineteen?'

'Yes. But I bet I know more about life than you do. I've been "out" some time you know—ever since I was sixteen.'

'Cleo, I think I'm in love with you.'

'I know, *mon ours*, I have eyes in my head. Do you want to marry me?'

Henry's Champagne, which he had been sipping furiously to calm his nerves, went down the wrong way. Cleo slapped him on the back.

'Well?'

'Of course I do. But it's fantastic. I could never marry you.'

'Why?'

'Well—your parents would never allow it.'

'To hell with them. They won't ever be able to stop me doing something I want to do.'

'Besides, you're rich, you're used to everything you want. I haven't any money. I haven't got a proper job. I don't even know what I want to do in life.'

'I don't care about money. Anyway, I could keep you by modelling. That is', she added sharply, 'if I chose to marry you.'

'Sir Rupert said you'd eat me alive.'

'Rupert's a timid old thing who's much too scared to take on a proper woman. I only eat up people who are already edible.'

'He said I'm not tough enough for you.'

'If you aren't, I won't have you. That's a promise.'

'As a matter of fact, what I said about having no money isn't quite correct. I think you've had a good effect on me already, Cleo. When I realized I was in love with you, I thought "I must make a lot of money, so I can marry her." So I got some, and put it all on a horse —something I've never done before—and won 500,000 francs.'

'Darling, how clever. And all for me? I think that's the nicest thing I've ever heard.' She put down her Champagne-glass, ran over to him, and kissed him—this time full on the mouth. He kissed her back, fiercely, pressing his tongue between her soft, full lips.

'No.' She pushed him back. 'We've got to talk first.'

'All right.'

'My papa wants me to marry somebody—the idiot son of some dreadful air force general he's conspiring with. I was sent down into the country to meet him. I

163

thought it better to obey, at this stage, and lie low. That's why I haven't been able to get in touch with you.'

'But Cleo, this is terrible——'

'Wait a minute. The boy is a fool of course. I pretended I quite liked him, to keep Papa happy, but said I hadn't made my mind up yet. He thinks he can persuade me into it. But while I was down there, staying at the general's château, I got to know a bit more about their schemes. Also, I had an idea. The boy's an expert with tape-recorders and so on. I said I was interested, and he showed me how to fix up a secret microphone connected to a recorder. So I ordered one from the Galeries Lafayette when I got back—I told Honor I needed it for speech-training. Look.'

She opened a shoe-locker at the bottom of a built-in wardrobe. Inside was a small tape recorder.

'It's connected to a tiny microphone in Papa's library. That's what I've been doing for the past two days—fixing it. It took me ages, because I had to hang around until the coast was clear. You see, I want to get an actual record of what my father and his friends are plotting. But it doesn't seem to be working properly yet. Papa was in there with Soustelle earlier this evening, so I switched it on. But all I got was a low murmur of voices—I've just been playing it back while I was waiting for you. I think perhaps the mike's in the wrong position.'

Henry looked at the recorder. 'But you've got the volume turned down', he said. 'Switch it to maximum.'

'Of course. How stupid of me not to notice it. Let's play it through again.'

This time they caught a few words and phrases—'integration . . . De Gaulle . . . the third parachute brigade . . . Léon can handle that . . . Lacoste . . . with us . . .' No coherent picture emerged, but it was un-mistakably the language of violence and revolution.

'My God', said Henry. 'You're quite right about these people. They're planning a *coup d'état.*'

'Of course they are', said Cleo impatiently. 'Now this is what I'm going to do. As soon as I can get a proper tape of one of their discussions, I shall get it to *L'Humanité.* They can make a transcript and put it all over their front page, with the tape as proof. The republican parties have a vague idea what my father is up to, but they're much too frightened of him and his friends in Algeria to put him under arrest. But if we could carry this through, they'd be bound to take action. There would be a tremendous swing in public opinion.'

'I wonder if you're right. A great many people I've talked to seem hostile to the Republic. They might be glad to see it destroyed. And you heard those people to-night when Soustelle came into the room?'

'They're just society lice. Of course they'd like a dictatorship here. Then they could crack down on the workers. Anyway, my idea is worth trying. Are you game?'

'Where do I come in?'

'In re-positioning the mike, to begin with. It obviously isn't in the right place. We're only catching a few words. I've put it behind one of the bookshelves, but we'll have to put it somewhere in the middle of the room. Under the desk, probably. And we must do it to-night.'

'*To-night?*'

'Yes—the sooner the better. Besides, you're already in the house, and that saves a lot of complications. We'll lie low here until all the guests have gone and everyone's in bed. Then we'll go down and fix it. I can do it, but I must have you to hold the torch—we can't risk putting on a light.'

'But how will I get out of the house afterwards? Is somebody always on duty at the gates?'

'Yes, unfortunately. You'll have to climb out of my window here. It overlooks the side-street leading off the road in front of the house. It's not a very big drop, and perhaps we can rig up a rope with sheets and things. Don't look so glum. Are you scared?'

'No—I mean yes. This is all very well for you. If you get caught, you simply have a row with your parents. But if they catch me, I'm in serious trouble. I could be prosecuted for interference in French internal affairs. They'd probably send me to gaol.'

Cleo sat down next to Henry on the sofa, seized his hands and stared at him hard. 'Henry, do you love me?'

'Of course I do. I wouldn't be here if I didn't. But why do we have to get mixed up in all this? Why can't we just go off together?'

'But that's just the point. I think perhaps I love you. But I won't know until I'm sure that you *care*. Don't you see? I care about things desperately, and when I care I want to *do* something. I despise people who just sit back and let things happen. I could never, never marry a man like that.'

'But *I* care, too.'

'Do you? I think you probably do. You're generous and kind-hearted, and you hate cruel people, and you'd like to see the world a better place to live in. But are you any more than that? Aren't you just one of those nice, liberal Englishmen who hold the right sort of views, and read the right sort of papers, and sign petitions against the South African Treason Trials, and deplore violence and torture and war, but who aren't actually prepared to go down into the streets and *fight* for what you believe?'

'That's not fair', said Henry hotly. 'During the Suez crisis, I marched in the procession to Downing Street. I was right in the middle of things. My umbrella was broken——'

'I know, I know. I was in London at the time. I went to Trafalgar Square, too. But it was just a great big demonstration of educated middle-class solidarity. I bet all your friends thought exactly like you—it was the thing to demonstrate against Suez. That didn't take courage. What I'm talking about is acting, on your own responsibility, as an *individual*, when you're not protected by a prevailing climate of opinion. Are you prepared to fight by yourself—and take the lead? I'm not just talking about politics, I'm talking about everything. Are you somebody who directs life, or is just carried along by it?'

'Yes, I see what you mean', said Henry. 'And the answer is, I don't know. It's funny you should ask these questions—I've often asked them myself. In a sense, I came to live in Paris to find out the answers. And perhaps I'm beginning to find them already. The life I've been leading would have horrified me a few weeks ago. But I almost think I'm beginning to like it. It's as though I'd started to acquire a taste for excitement.'

Cleo leaned over and kissed him, lightly. 'Then you'll help me?'

'Yes, dammit. But I don't trust you an inch, Cleo. You know you're beautiful and that I'm in love with you. I think you're just using me, as the nearest available male, and that when you've finished with me I'll be thrown away like an old cigarette packet.'

'Not true. You shall see. We've got hours yet before the house settles down. I'll show you I can love, too.' She moved towards him on the sofa and kissed him again, this time lingering on his lips and twining her arms round his neck.

To go to bed, for the first time, with a beautiful woman with whom you are in love, is always, in a sense, an ordeal; it is far more terrifying if it takes place in her parents' house, and as a prelude to a conspiracy against them. Yet, as Henry began to caress her breasts, warm and firm under their satin skin, to run his hands over her thighs, to feel her warm, compact body pressed against his, a feeling of confidence gradually blossomed inside him. The undertone of fear, based on guilt, which had dominated his previous love-making with women, had quite disappeared. What he was doing seemed unarguably right, and therefore easy and instinctive.

'Shall I unfasten my dress?' whispered Cleo.

'No. Let me do it', said Henry. His hands did not tremble, his fingers were light and skilful. The dress cascaded into a silky sea at her feet. Underneath she wore only the tiniest brassiere, and a narrow black triangle round her loins. The soft lamplight gilded her skin, as though a thousand candles glowed underneath.

A few seconds later, she lay in the vast four-poster bed, watching Henry while he undressed. He had turned out all the lights save one, in the far corner of the room: it was reflected in the dark pools of her eyes, which seemed, for the first time since he had known her, timid and uncertain.

He slipped under the sheets—they were silk and already warm from her body—and stretched out a hand towards her. She lay stiff and silent on her back, and his caressing fingers evoked no response. He felt her shiver.

'What's the matter, darling?' he asked. 'Are you afraid of me?'

'You'll be kind to me, Henry, won't you?' Her voice was almost inaudible.

'But of course I will, darling.' His hand touched one of her breasts, so gently that he could scarcely feel the smooth, warm skin under his finger-tips. And suddenly she flung herself into his arms, pressing her body violently against his, her lips against his ear, her heart pounding against his chest. She was sobbing.

'Oh, darling, you do understand, don't you?' she said, clinging desperately to him. 'I've never done this before. I'm so silly to behave like this, but I'm so scared and I want you to make love to me so much.'

'But, Cleo, I had no idea. I thought——'

'I know. It's all my fault. I pretend I'm sophisticated, and I know I've made all the advances with you. You think I'm a woman of the world, but I'm not at all really, just silly and frightened. But I think I do love you, and I want you—oh, so much.'

Henry had never slept with a virgin before, and the idea conjured up a fresh galaxy of fears and uncertainties. There was, however, only one thing to do—only one thing that he wanted to do—and he did it. It was not easy, for Henry was inexperienced and Cleo, at any rate to begin with, clumsy with terror. But gradually, he felt his confidence and sense of mastery returning, gradually her groans yielded to little cries of pleasure, and her flesh began to respond: the moment even came when they were totally one, just as they had been when Henry first saw her in the Louvre, isolated from a world that had ceased to exist. A few seconds later she was asleep in his arms, and this time Henry, too, slept.

Her stirrings awoke him, after what seemed an infinity. She sat up and switched on the light by the side of the bed, studying the gold hands of the little ivory-cased clock which stood on the bedside table. There was absolute silence in the house.

'Three o'clock.' She kissed him, long, lingeringly. 'Darling, now I know I love you.'

'We must dress and go downstairs', Henry found himself saying. 'It'll be daylight in less than three hours.' For the first time, he was giving orders.

'Yes.' She slipped out of bed, crossed to a wardrobe and put on a pair of trousers and a woollen sweater. Henry gathered up his scattered evening clothes and began to dress. The room was chilly after the warm comforts of Cleo's bed.

'I've remembered I left my overcoat with the butler. I must get it, or somebody will find it odd.'

'Yes. I know where it'll be. We can get it on the way back.' She had unearthed a small selection of screwdrivers and wire-cutters, a coil of flex, and a large electric torch. 'Are you ready?'

'Yes!'

Cleo unlocked the door slowly, and they tip-toed along the corridor and down the stairs. Fortunately, Madame Plympton's passion for thick carpets made their progress completely silent. The library was at the other end of the house, on the ground floor, and they gained it without difficulty, though its heavy, oak-panelled door creaked painfully as they went inside. Cleo's torch picked out the corner of the high bookshelves where her microphone was concealed.

'I put it behind a volume of Bossuet's sermons', she whispered. 'I knew he'd never read them.'

'You mean to say', said Henry, 'you fixed a wire all this way from your bedroom?'

'Yes. Along the picture rail for the most part. Now help me with this step-ladder while I get it down.'

It took them nearly two hours, working feverishly. First Cleo had to unscrew the microphone. Then she had to connect up a fresh length of flex with the terminal. They had to remove, and replace, great quantities of books, so that the wire could be brought to the floor down the back of the book-shelves, which fortunately fitted loosely. Next, they rolled back the carpet and replaced it with the flex underneath. But how to get it from under the carpet to the underside of the desk, which they had chosen as the best place to fix the microphone?

'We'll have to bore a hole in the carpet and bring it up through that', said Henry. 'But that'll mean pushing back the desk.'

'*Merde!* It's enormous.'

They struggled together with the vast desk, which had once been in Saint-Beuve's room at the Institut. It moved, eventually, about a foot, but not before Henry had slipped on the carpet, and involuntarily struck the side of the desk with the palm of his hand.

'Don't worry', said Cleo. 'They won't hear that upstairs.'

'Now for the carpet', said Henry. To drive a hole through it was more easily imagined than done: it had a thick pile, and there was a foamy rubber coating underneath. Jabbing and prodding with a screwdriver was no good. And they had no sharp boring tool.

'Have you any matches?' asked Cleo.

'Yes', said Henry, feeling in his pockets.

'Then let's burn a hole.'

Henry lit a match and held it against the spot. It singed the surface of the carpet, and went out, producing little result except a strong smell of burning.

'More', said Cleo. Henry lit another match.

Twenty-five matches and ten minutes later, the surface of the carpet had been scorched and frayed so threadbare that the rubber lining began to show through. That, too, emitted a nauseating smell. Henry felt sweat trickling down his back and chest.

'Somebody's going to think the house is on fire', he whispered fiercely. 'I daren't try any more matches. Let's have another go with the screwdriver.'

Five minutes later, they were through, and Cleo rapidly pushed the flex to Henry. They inched the desk back into place. It was enclosed on three sides, so that unless the Fouette housemaids were exceptionally conscientious—which Cleo claimed they were not—the hole, flex and microphone would not be noticed until the carpet was next cleaned.

'Now to fix the mike', said Cleo. 'You hold the torch and hand me the screws.' She squirmed her way under the desk, and Henry followed suit. This was the really tricky part, for though the desk was vast, the space was still confined. Cleo, moreover, was showing signs of fatigue: the strain of pushing the desk had made her arms tremble, and she found it increasingly difficult to insert the screws which held the flex and microphone in place.

'Let me take over', said Henry. 'You step out for a second and stretch your legs.'

Cleo obeyed, and Henry wriggled into her place. A

second later he heard a thunderous, reverberating crash. Cleo, stepping backwards, had upset a rack of steel fire-irons which stood in the fireplace, a few feet behind the desk; and they in turn had clanged against a copper fire-screen.

'God!' said Henry. 'They're bound to hear that.'

'Not necessarily', said Cleo, with an effort at calmness, though there was a hint of tension in her voice. 'They won't have heard it upstairs, and old Boule, the night porter, is the only one who sleeps on this floor. He's a heavy sleeper, too. Give me a hand to put these things on their feet again.'

Together they put back the fire-irons, and Henry once more crawled under the desk, Cleo holding the torch. He didn't take much trouble with the screws: at the most, they'd only have to last a few weeks. Twenty minutes later, flex and microphone were in place.

'That's it.' said Henry. 'We've done it!'

'Quiet. Somebody's coming.' She switched off the torch, and in the darkness he could feel her body tense. She crawled a little further under the desk, so they were both wedged up together, breathing the acrid smell of singed carpet, which still lingered.

Cleo had heard the sound of footsteps on the marble floor of the hall. But the corridor outside the library was carpeted, and the first they knew—as they waited and listened—of the stranger's approach, was when the door swung open, and a voice said: '*Qui est là?*' Then there was silence. Cleo handed Henry the wire-cutters, which had a long, heavy, cast-iron handle. The implication of the gesture was obvious, and Henry, despite himself, shivered. He had never hit anyone with a blunt instrument before.

The figure advanced a few paces into the room, then the lights were switched on. Fortunately, Henry and Cleo were entirely concealed from his line of vision, for the desk faced the door.

'*Personne*', muttered the figure, in an elderly voice—it was old Boule, evidently. Then followed another pause, and Henry distinctly heard the sound of sniffing. He had caught the smell of burning! Cleo's hand stretched out and gripped his wrist tightly. Boule's footsteps on the soft carpet could not be heard; but the sound of his sniffs drew nearer, until they were within a foot or two of the desk. Henry picked up his wire-cutters.

For a full minute, the old man sniffed and sniffed. But his sense of smell was no longer accurate enough to guide him to the exact spot. A smell of burning is a very elusive thing, and after further sniffings at the opposite end of the room, he left, switching out the lights and closing the door. Henry picked up the torch and shone it on Cleo's face. It was beautiful in relief, as in fear, as in anything. He kissed her gently, and she clung to him.

'Thank God you were here', she whispered. 'Otherwise I know I'd have screamed. Oh, thank God I've got you.'

'We must wait five minutes or so, and then go back', said Henry. 'It's practically five o'clock, and it begins to get light at half-past.'

In the five minutes, they took a careful survey of the room, to ensure they had left nothing and that everything was in its place.

'My overcoat', said Henry.

'Yes, I hadn't forgotten. It'll be in the cloakroom near the hall. I'd better get it alone, just in case old Boule is still up and prowling. You go back up into my room in the meantime—you know the way.'

Henry regained Cleo's bedroom without incident, shut the door carefully, then crossed to the window through which he would have to make his get-away. No street-lamps burned, and the night was pitch dark. He could see nothing whatsoever, and there was no indication how deep the drop was: to judge by the height of the ground-floor rooms, not less than twenty feet.

'Look here', he said, when Cleo returned, carrying his coat, 'I can't see a damn thing out there. I'll have to have some sort of rope.'

'I've got one', said Cleo triumphantly. 'Look—I found it in the cloakroom, next to the fire extinguishers.' It was a half-inch coil, about thirty feet in length, which she had concealed under his coat.

'Good girl.' Henry tied one end firmly to a post on the bed, then tested it by lying on his back, putting his feet against the base of the bed, and pulling with all his strength. The massive old four-poster refused to move an inch. He then uncoiled the rope out of the window and felt it touch bottom.

'Right, I'm ready to go now.' She helped him into his coat, and kissed him, clinging tightly to him, her arms around his waist. 'When shall I hear from you, Cleo?'

'Tomorrow. Or the day after. It's too dangerous for us to meet, I think. Quite a lot of people in Paris know me.'

'Lunch with me the day after tomorrow. We can go to somewhere quiet on the other side of the city.'

'I'll try. I'll telephone you tomorrow.'

'Right. Goodbye.'

'Take care, darling.'

Henry dangled his leg over the edge of the window-frame, gripped the rope with his legs and hands, and slid cautiously down. Behind him, Cleo had re-drawn the curtains, so that no chink of light should reveal his presence to anyone in the street. For the first few feet, Henry found the going quite easy, then the strain on his arms and legs began to tell. His slippery evening shoes lost their grip on the rope entirely, and he found himself dangling precariously by his arms alone. Suddenly, his feet touched ground—or at any rate, some sort of obstacle. He tapped it with one of his feet, and the sound was mysterious—faintly metallic, he thought. He probed around with both feet, planted them firmly, and slowly relaxed the weight on his arms and stood up. Then he lowered himself on to his hands and knees, and crawled forward. The plane on which he was placed—it was certainly metallic—came to an abrupt end after he had advanced about three feet. He gingerly stretched out a leg, and his foot encountered another plane, about eighteen inches further below. Was he on some sort of shed? And if so, why hadn't Cleo warned him it was there? The lower plane seemed somewhat narrower, but in any other direction there were precipitous depths, so Henry wriggled himself, bottom forward, on to it, and began to crawl along again. This, too, came to an abrupt end, and Henry banged his knee painfully on a sharp object, a few inches high, which projected from the smooth surface. He stretched out his hand to rub his knee, lost his balance, rolled off the plane, and landed heavily on what was obviously the street, three feet below. Exasperated, he decided to risk striking a match, shielding it carefully with his hand. From his sitting position on the street, all he could see was a huge wheel. He stood up, peering closer. A polished radiator came into view, surmounted by the silvery outline of the

Winged Victory. He had landed on top of Madame Plympton's Rolls-Royce.

The match burned itself out and Henry began to advance cautiously along the side of the house, which at this point jutted out into the alleyway, concealing any view of the main street. At last he turned the corner, and saw with relief the pale, reflected glow of the street lamps. He walked now at a normal pace, and turned sharply right when he reached the street. Somewhere in the direction he was heading, he knew, there was a square where there might be all-night taxis.

Fifty yards on, however, he heard footsteps a long way behind him, faint but gaining. He walked faster.

A voice said: '*Qui est là? Arrêtez-vous!*'

Even without turning round, Henry knew it must be a policeman. With a house so full of loot as the Plympton-la Fouette's, there was probably one on duty outside all night. Henry began to run, fast, turned the corner, and plunged downhill along a street of shuttered shops. His feet echoed wildly on the pavement, and he was unable to hear whether the policeman was following him or not, At the corner of the Place Neuport he paused for breath. and to listen. Yes: he could still hear the footsteps.

Then, out of the gloom, came the bulky shape of a battered old Renault taxi. It had no lights, apart from its headlamps, but Henry dashed into the street and hailed it.

'*Mais vous voyez, monsieur*—I have a hat on my flag. I'm going home to the Porte de la Villette.'

Henry waved a bunch of thousand franc notes. 'Five thousand to take me to the Boulevard St. Germain', he said, trying to keep an hysterical edge out of his voice.

The driver stared hard at him for about five seconds,

cocked his ear, heard the distant sound of footsteps, noted Henry's dinner jacket and black bow tie, then flung open the door. The engine revved, he let in the clutch, and the huge old monster trundled forward.

'One is pursuing you', he said over his shoulder. 'At half past five in the morning, that can be only one of two people—a policeman or a husband. *Mais la police ne s'occupe pas des gens en smoking.*'

'*C'est ça*', said Henry, relaxing against the cushions.

A taxi is like the womb. To anyone anxious to hurry away from something unpleasant, it offers the release of responsibility, the security of flight: one is in a small, dark, comfortable protected world. Reflecting on this, Henry dozed gently as he rattled on towards the Left Bank.

The next day, Saturday, brought no message from Cleo. Nor did Sunday. Henry spent an apprehensive week-end, leaving the hotel only for meals, in the hope that he would be summoned to the telephone. His hanging about plainly irritated Madame Marcourt; so did his anxious enquiries if there were any messages for him, each time he returned. Her negatives became progressively more abrupt and hostile. Indeed, her attitude towards him, which had been commercially effusive before the visit of the plain-clothes detective, was now distinctly suspicious. And it appeared to be shared by the other inmates of the hotel. Madame Salbert, for instance, who had been embarrassingly forthcoming at one stage, now cut him dead. Even the elderly Communist deputy, M. Hurlot, gave him only the briefest of nods when they met on the stairs. There were no more invitations to coffee.

Henry arrived at his office on Monday morning in a sombre mood. The crisis still dragged on. M. Pleven had failed to form a government; other old political wheel-horses were having a try. The Parisians seemed uninterested, though some of the student gangs were making their appearance on the streets again. The weather was hot, though overcast, and for the first time that year the typists, hurrying to work, were wearing cotton frocks. Henry found Francie and Regina in emancipated mood.

'Good morning, Sir', said Francie.

'Chief', corrected Regina.

'What's the idea?' asked Henry, irritably.

'Rupert', said Francie, 'has suddenly decided to go on holiday. He left yesterday, and sent a message to my hotel. It reads: "Darling Francie, must go to Spain for two weeks or so until the crisis is over. Can't stand all the boring conversations about it here. Please see that my rascally valet attends to my laundry. Charles of course will be in charge of the paper. Love, Rupert". So there you are. Have you any commands?'

'Yes', said Henry. 'How is this paper of ours coming along, anyway? We don't seem to have heard from the printers for days.'

'Here it is', said Francie triumphantly, holding up a copy. 'The new issue's finished—it arrived from the printers this morning.'

'Tell him the worst', said Regina.

'Oh, yes. There are one of two minor er—imperfections, I guess. The big colour photograph of the new French airliner has been printed upside down. And one or two captions seem to have got mixed up.'

'President Coty', said Regina, 'is described as a new

oil refinery near Marseilles. And the refinery has turned up in the article on *pâté de foie gras* in the cook-book section.'

'How could this possibly happen?' asked Henry.

'Well', said Francie, 'we must have pasted up the dummies wrong, and of course none of the printers know any English. This sort of thing occurs from time to time, you know. Sometimes we get puzzled letters from subscribers.'

'Well, see that it doesn't happen again', said Henry severely.

'Yes, Sir. By the way, Madame Plympton has sent her article for the new issue.'

'O.K., I'll take it', said Henry. 'Anything else?'

'Yes. You had a mysterious personal long-distance call from Normandy. A lady, but wouldn't give her name. Said she'd call back.'

Henry's heart missed a beat. 'I'll take the call in Rupert's office.'

'I see', said Francie archly, 'so that we can't hear what you say to her.'

'Exactly', said Henry, going into the inner office and shutting the door. The call, he guessed, must have come from Cleo. But why was she in Normandy? Had anything gone wrong? Perhaps the microphone had been found, and traced to her room. He waited anxiously while the minutes ticked by, and in an effort to calm his nerves, began to read Madame Plympton's new article— an adulative profile of the Gaullist leaders which she had entitled 'The Coming Men in France'. The grammar was a little worse than before, the sentiments considerably more nauseating. Henry edited it in the most perfunctory fashion, deliberately leaving in two double negatives, a defective gerund and five misspellings. This eased his conscience a little, but not much.

The call came through at eleven-thirty. Cleo sounded calm, but worried.

'Darling, I'm sorry I couldn't reach you before.'

'Where are you speaking from?'

'Near Falaise. My papa has a château here. I was ordered down on Saturday morning, and I thought it was the best policy to obey. Do you still love me, darling?'

'Of course I do. What are you doing down there?'

'Philippe—that's the Air Force general's son—has been invited down. My parent's idea is that this visit should clinch the match. Apparently, the general's proving a bit slow about joining in their scheme, and wants to make sure his son is hitched up to a substantial heiress—that's me—in case something goes wrong, and he's dismissed from his post.'

'God!'

'So I think they'll keep me down here until I say yes. The trouble is, the wretched boy follows me around all the time. I can't telephone from the château, and this morning's the first opportunity I've had of getting to a call-box alone. Darling, you must advise me what to do.'

'How do you mean?'

'Well, I must get back to Paris. Otherwise I can't do anything, and there'll be no point in having fixed up the mike—I've got to be there to operate it. Papa went back to Paris with my stepmother this morning, no doubt for more plotting. But if I don't tell Philippe I'll marry him, I'll be stuck down here indefinitely. You see?'

'Why don't you catch the first train to Paris, meet me here, and we'll go to London.'

'*No*, Henry. That means giving all our plans up. We

must go through with this. I *knew* you didn't care.' She sounded tearful.

'Blast it, of course I care. But I care far more about you than I do about any French government. Let them be beastly to each other in their own way. I want to take you out of this bloody country.'

'Henry, I know you love me. But I want a man who does more than just love me. I want him to be a man that *matters*. You've got to make yourself matter, Henry— and that means imposing yourself on society. Oh, God— I'm talking just like a newspaper article.'

'All right, then this is my advice. Tell the boy you'll agree to an engagement, but insist that you don't know him well enough yet, and that it'll have to be a long one. Then you can come back to Paris without really committing yourself.'

'Yes, I think that's right. But, Henry, suppose he wants to kiss me?'

'Then *let* him', said Henry, struggling to control himself. 'But for God's sake get back to Paris. I'm getting nervous with all this waiting. Why doesn't this crisis blow up, anyway?'

'It will—at the end of this week. I think they'll form a government, and Papa is angling for a job in it. The republicans will probably give it to him, in the hope that it will pacify the extremists. But in fact, it's only so that he can get hold of a government department and use official cyphers and things. Darling, I don't think we're going to win this.'

'It doesn't matter. Please don't worry. We'll do our best.'

'I must go now. I'll try and get in touch as soon as I get back.'

The line went dead, in the mysterious way French telephones have. Henry went into the outer office and handed Madame Plympton's article to Francie.

'I've done this. Phone her and tell her to send a messenger round to collect it, and return it this afternoon. If she wants to know why I can't bring it round myself, tell her I'm too busy.'

'Henry, is that wise?'

'Yes. And now I'm going out to lunch.'

He walked down the Rue de Bourgogne and into the Place du Palais Bourbon. A small crowd had gathered near the entrance to the Assemblée Nationale, where the deputies were arriving and departing in large black Citroëns. There were a few cries of *Vive de Gaulle!* and *Les Députés à la lanterne!* The policemen who guarded the gates made no attempt to interfere.

'They're not really worth bothering about, the French, are they?' said a voice at Henry's elbow. It was, of course, Edgar, looking surprisingly *boulevardier* in a new dark-blue suit. 'Who would die for the Fourth Republic?'

'Democracy's always worth dying for', said Henry sharply, somewhat to his own surprise. Cleo's telephone exhortation was still much on his mind.

'It all depends on the angle of vision', said Edgar loftily. 'You, as a proletarian wage-slave, employed on dubious work by a bourgeois government, naturally believe passionately in universal suffrage. While I, as a capitalist, would tend to take a different view.'

'A capitalist?'

'Haven't you heard? My—er—publisher has taken me into partnership. At my insistence, I may add. I discovered that my *livres galants* were selling so well that I was in a position to strike a bargain with him. I threat-

183

ened to write no more, unless he gave me a share of the profits. The poor man had to capitulate.'

'So you've left the Party?'

'By no means. I have merely acquired a coin of vantage within the capitalist system the better to strike it a mortal blow when the time comes. As I told you before. I have also acquired a mistress.'

'Really?'

'Indeed. None other than our mutual acquaintance, Lady Treffle.'

'Dora?' Henry found, to his relief, that he could laugh without embarrassment at the mention of her name. 'Then what became of Crick? Did she ditch him?'

'Alas, no. Rather the reverse. He's taken up with an American lady of means, and is now living at the Georges Cinq Hotel. You see, we are all moving up in the world.'

'And have you stopped writing poetry?'

'Of course not. My vocation remains unchanged. Indeed, success seems to be smiling on it. Next month I have been asked by Associated Network Television to read my poems on their "Youth at the Helm" programme. They're flying me to London for the performance. I shall appear in the now, unfortunately, conventional role of an angry young man, and read them "The Prole's Last Wish", "Wall Street Rock", and "Epitaph on a Murdered Algerian". Dora, who, as you know, was once an actress of sorts, will also appear, reciting my "Lament of a Call-Girl After Reading the Wolfenden Report". Nor is this all. The Royal Court Theatre is at the moment considering my political farce, "Up in Mac's Room", and I daily await a summons to luncheon at Buckingham Palace. My literary image, in fact, is beginning to take shape: I see myself as a Betjeman of the Left.'

As Edgar talked, a black Buick swung into the courtyard of the Assembly. In the back seat, relaxed against the cushions, was the Count.

'There goes my future father-in-law', said Henry.

'Niki la Fouette? A tiresome man. Always plotting away and making noisy speeches about patriotism. A Pétainist, of course. But does this mean you've won the curvaceous Cleo? If so, my congratulations. Her stepmother, I believe, will cut up for fifty million, and Cleo should get a substantial slice. Beauty is important in a bride, but so is wealth—especially to a young man of the Left.

> Sweeter than ruby lips
> Fairer than silken flank
> Nicer than swinging hips
> Is money in the bank.

'What nonsense you talk', said Henry. 'Even if the marriage goes through, I shan't get a *sou*. Her parents don't know anything about it, and would certainly take action if they did. As a matter of fact, they're determined to marry her to the son of some awful Air Force general, who's going to help Fouette take over the country.'

'Ah, yes. That will be General Maurice. He's the Superintendant of Air Staff in the Paris District, which controls all the military airfields. Fouette and his friends will need him if they're to land paratroopers from Algiers.'

'Look, Edgar, how do you know all this?'

'Through the firm. My partner, Skorsky, has all sorts of intimate contacts with the great. He's currently publishing a Lesbian novel, written under a pseudonym by the wife of an ex-Prime Minister, for instance. He tells me all the gossip.'

'Well, if you hear anything, let me know. Cleo and I have a rather personal interest in the outcome of this crisis.'

'Certainly, dear boy. And now I must be off to join Dora. We're lunching at the Tour d'Argent.'

No news came from Cleo for a week. For want of anything better to do, Henry devoted himself to the office. Orders had come from Maxim that in view of the crisis the next issue was to be rushed through, and Henry spent many hours correcting proofs. The crisis grew steadily worse. On 13th May, the army took power in Algiers and called for the formation of a government of national safety, led by General De Gaulle. That evening, the republican parties of the Assembly voted into office by a large majority a government led by M. Pflimlin. Henry noted that M. Nicol la Fouette (Independent) had been appointed Minister for Economic Co-ordination. The *Figaro* announced that, as a consequence of threats to assassinate him by Algerian terrorists, he had been given a large police guard and his family were under police protection at his château in Normandy. This, no doubt, would explain Cleo's silence.

Two days later, M. Soustelle, who had been placed under house arrest, escaped and joined the insurgents in Algeria. The revolt spread to Corsica. It became known that the government had entered into negotiations with De Gaulle. Paris began to fill with steel-helmeted riot troops and journalists.

On Thursday, when Henry arrived at his office, he

found a *pneumatique* waiting for him. It read simply:
'Darling, have at last got back. Meet me in the Crillon
Bar at twelve-thirty without fail. Love, Cleo.'

Henry got to the hotel five minutes early, and fought
his way to the bar, jammed two-deep with the broad
backs of Special Correspondents. The air was loud with
prophecy.

'De Gaulle's going to hold a press conference to-night.'

' . . . to-morrow.'

'Sunday . . .'

' . . . this afternoon, four-thirty.'

'I hear he's looking his age. He can hardly hold a pen
to sign his name . . .'

'Fit as a fiddle.'

'Gaga'.

'Five triple whiskies, George.'

' . . . Soustelle escaped in a trunk.'

'A laundry basket, actually . . .'

'Disguised as a woman.'

'Dressed as a policeman . . .'

'In a Black Maria . . .'

' . . . on a bicycle . . .'

'Fill 'em up, George.'

'Pineau told me . . .'

' . . . as I said to Mollet. Listen Guy, I said . . .'

'Two battalions of infantry in the Bois . . .'

' . . . sixteen tanks hidden in the Champs Elysées . . .'

'A fighter squadron over Toulouse . . .'

' . . . aircraft cariers off Marseilles.'

'Bottoms up, Joe. *Vive la République*, what?'

'Cheers. Up the Frogs!'

'*Skol!*'

'*Salud!*'

'Gentlemen, we are witnessing a unique moment of history . . .'

' . . . the beginning of an era.'

'The end of an epoch . . .'

' . . . the opening of a new chapter.'

'A fresh page in the dramatic story of France.'

'Seven quadruple whiskies, George. *Avec beaucoup de* soda, old boy.'

Henry sat down at one of the tables and sipped a *citron pressé*. He saw Cleo the moment she entered the swing door, but watched her silently as she struggled through the crowd, her eyes anxious, her colour high, her hair loose over the collar of her saffron linen coat. Then their eyes met, and the uncertainties of the last week disappeared.

'Darling', said Cleo. 'What a struggle it was to get here. We only arrived back from the country last night. Papa wanted to keep us down there, but Honor blew her top. She said she wasn't going to miss the chance to make history just for the sake of a few Ay-rabs. So he gave way. But I have a detective following me around all the time.'

'Good Lord! Is he here now?'

'No. He's outside. He wanted to come in, but I hinted it was an *affaire de cœur*, so he gave me a wink and stationed himself at the door.'

'Darling, I think we've lost.'

'Probably. But there's one chance—the Paris workers. If they can be mobilized, I don't think they'd dare land paratroops.'

'But they don't seem to care. They're just going to work as though nothing was happening.'

'I know. We've got to administer a shock. Listen. Papa's having another gathering of his friends tonight, before dinner. I think they're going to co-ordinate the paratroop landings on Paris with Algiers. Philippe's father—you know, the General—will be there. I shall take a tape of their conversation. I want you to come and collect it about ten tonight and take it to C.P. headquarters in the Carrefour de Châteaudun. They can make a transcript and publish the lot in tomorrow's *L'Humanité*.'

'But how can I get into your house?'

'That's the problem. Couldn't you pretend you'd come to collect one of Honor's articles?'

Henry thought for a few seconds. 'Yes, I could. I've got her article in proof at the office. I could send it round this afternoon, and say I'd collect it after dinner, because it has to go to the printer first thing tomorrow morning.'

'Yes—and then I can slip the tape into the packet. So when you come, don't ask for me. Just say you've come for the article.'

'But what about getting into the party headquarters? I don't know anybody there. Don't you think it would be wise to take Pierre-Emile with me?'

'Didn't you know? He was arrested yesterday. They had a big round-up of students—fascists, Communists, everyone on the black-list.'

'I see. So what do I do—ask for Arpad?'

'Yes. Say you're bringing a message from me. I must go now. Darling, do you still want to marry me?'

'You know I do. Why do you ask?'

'Because you're probably going to have to. As soon as I see we get this stuff in L'*Humanité*, I'm going to make a dash for it. I've already packed a suitcase. So wait for me at your hotel tomorrow morning.'

'Darling, I'll wait for you anywhere.'

She kissed him. 'Don't look so tragically heroic. And keep your fingers crossed. Goodbye.' She vanished into the forest of journalistic backs, and Henry once more became conscious of the world around him.

'... machine-guns on the roof of the Assembly.'

'Reminds me of Hungary. . . .'

'... Korea.'

'Saigon. . . .'

'Madrid.'

'OK, George, fill 'em up again, *mon vieux*. . . .'

Henry had never engaged in a political conspiracy before, and he was, therefore, unduly pessimistic about its outcome. But all seemed to go well. Francie sent the page-proofs of Madame Plympton's article round in the afternoon, and arranged for it to be collected by Henry at ten. He arrived by taxi at the house dead on time, was admitted through the gates, and handed a packet by the butler. It felt satisfactorily bulky. Once back in the taxi, he tore it open, and found the spool of tape, the article, and a note from Cleo. He read it by the intermittent lights of the street-lamps as they rattled towards the Carrefour du Châteaudun. It said simply: 'It's all here, I think. Dates, times, places, number of troops, signals, and most of the names. The mike worked beautifully. Please don't fail. Am looking desperately forward to tomorrow. All my love, Cleo.'

Henry stopped the taxi just before they came to the Carrefour, in case the driver should remember him as visiting C.P. headquarters. He waited until the taxi had driven off, then walked briskly across the street towards the massive concrete building. Lights blazed in the higher storeys, but the windows of the ground floor were covered with thick steel shutters. Over the entrance hung a limp banner which read: *'Paix, Pain et Liberté'*. As Henry approached the big bronze doors, two bulky figures stationed themselves in front of him.

'Your business, comrade?'

'I want to see Monsieur Arpad.'

'Come inside.'

One of the men led him to a desk in the ground-floor lobby. A grim middle-aged receptionist, with a Stalinist hair-style, telephoned up to Arpad's office.

'He wants to know what you want to see him about', she said to Henry.

'Tell him I have an important message from Mademoiselle La Fouette.'

'Monsieur Arpad says he is in conference, but will receive you in five minutes.'

One of the guards took Henry up the lift to the fourth floor, and into a bare, carpetless reception room. He gestured to a hard, wooden chair. Henry sat down, while the guard leaned against the door, smoking. He was kept waiting ten minutes. Then Arpad came out of the inner office, preceded by a dark, broad-shouldered man in a double-breasted blue suit. Henry thought he had seen his photograph in the papers. No doubt a member of the Central Committee. He shook Henry's hand.

'What have you brought from Comrade La Fouette?'

Henry handed him the tape. 'Fouette held a meeting at his house earlier this evening. They settled their final arrangements for landing paratroops round Paris. It's all recorded on this tape. We're giving it to you so you can publish it in *L'Humanité.*'

The official exchanged a glance with Arpad and smiled.

'This is not entirely news to us. We have our own sources of information. However, please convey our gratitude to the young lady.' He pocketed the tape and turned to go.

'Well', said Henry, 'are you going to publish it?'

'Alas, no. It is, in a sense, already out of date. No paratroops will land in Paris. The crisis is virtually over. De Gaulle will probably agree tomorrow to form a government.'

'Then all the more reason for publishing it', said Henry hotly. 'If the workers can be aroused, there's just a chance we can prevent De Gaulle from taking over.'

'And what makes you think that would be desirable?'

'Because he'll set up a fascist dictatorship', said Henry. 'It will be a victory for Soustelle and the *colons*. Your party has already said so.'

'To be sure. And we shall vote against De Gaulle's investiture. But there are compensations. De Gaulle may destroy a little of the freedom that is left to us in France. But he may restore to us the freedom we should enjoy in international affairs.'

'In other words, you're prepared to sacrifice the interests of the French workers at the dictate of Soviet foreign policy.'

'Soviet policy is always in the interests of workers everywhere. It is scarcely in the interests of French workers, is it, to be destroyed by hydrogen bombs?' He looked at his watch. 'However, I fear I do not have the time to engage in theoretical discussion with you, *jeune homme*.'

'You cynical bastard', said Henry in English. 'Then give me back the tape. I'll get it published somewhere else.'

'That will be impossible. I must now ask you to leave.' He made a gesture to the guard, who advanced towards Henry.

Henry leaped at the Communist leader, seizing him by the lapels of his suit. The man collapsed under the sudden force of the attack and they both rolled on the ground with Henry on top. The guard hurried over to them, attempting to smash his huge fist in Henry's face. Henry, who saw the blow coming, jerked his head to one side, and the fist landed square on the Communist leader's nose: there was the brittle snap of a broken bone and a sharp howl of pain. The guard, appalled, staggered back and Henry dived for his legs. He fell heavily, colliding with a massive mahogany hat-stand. Henry raced back to the groaning party boss, who was sitting upright, desperately trying to staunch the river of blood pouring from his nose. Henry plunged his hand into the pocket of the man's suit, and dragged out the tape. But the guard, who had got to his feet again, was on top of him: the tape slipped out of Henry's hand, spinning across the floor in a silver streak. The room suddenly became full of people: two men held Henry's arms twisted behind his back.

The Communist leader climbed slowly and painfully to his feet. 'Lock him up', he said, 'and keep him there. We'll decide what to do about him to-morrow.' He dabbed angrily at his nose with his handkerchief.

'You can't do this', shouted Henry. 'It's illegal—it's false imprisonment.' But the guards were already dragging him out into the corridor. He decided to hang limp, and wait his chance to escape. It came when they reached the lift. One of the guards held back the gates, while the other prepared to drag Henry in. With a sudden and violent lurch forward, he tore his arms free, plunged into the open lift and slammed across the gates. With one hand he held them shut; with the other he pressed the button marked *Rez de Chaussée*, and sank majestically downwards: for an instant, the guards gazed impotently at him, while he disappeared from sight, then they turned and dashed for the stairs.

There are only six express lifts in the whole of Paris, which boasts some of the slowest and most perilous lifts in the world. One of the six, however, happens to be in Communist Party headquarters: it brought Henry to the ground floor while the guards were still stamping heavily down the stairs leading to the second. He opened the gates, walked briskly through the lobby, nodding pleasantly to the grim receptionist, and pushed open the bronze doors. A policeman was walking along the pavement, and Henry approached him.

'Where's the nearest Métro?' he asked.

The policeman pointed. 'Across the other side of the Carrefour. You can't miss it.'

Henry thanked him, then glanced round at the doors of the building behind him. Through the glass partition, he saw the two guards, watching him with hopeless anger. He gave them a courteous wave, and strolled slowly over to the Métro.

Henry's successful escape had filled him with exhilaration. He was really beginning to enjoy this sort of life, he told himself. But as the train bumped and rattled towards St. Germain des Prés, his mood of self-satisfaction evaporated. He had failed in his mission. He had not even succeeded in recovering the tape. All Cleo's efforts had been wasted. The battle against the fascists was as good as lost, since even the Communists seemed reconciled to their victory. What were he and Cleo to do now? She had promised to join him at his hotel as soon as she saw the story in *L'Humanité*. Now it would not appear. They had made no alternative plans, foolishly, and to telephone her might be fatal. Henry suddenly felt very weary and discouraged.

He decided to return to his hotel and sleep on it. To-morrow, when he got to his office, he could think of some excuse to call at Madame Plympton's house—he could claim, for instance, that he had to cut her article and wanted her approval—and then try and get Cleo alone for a few seconds. It was not a very promising plan, but there seemed no other alternative. Twenty minutes later, he was asleep in bed, dreaming of confused struggles.

He was awoken, just after dawn, by a thunderous hammering on his door.

'Open up', said a voice. 'Police.'

Henry sat up sharply in bed, his thoughts racing. So it had come at last: arrest, imprisonment, disgrace. But with which of his now numerous felonious activities would he be charged? Escape was quite out of the question: his window opened onto a sheer drop of forty feet. He climbed slowly out of bed and began to put on his dressing-gown.

'Open up', said the voice again, louder. 'And don't try anything—we're armed.'

It was more serious than he had thought. Why should they think he was armed? But perhaps this was just the characteristic French tendency towards hysterical exaggeration. He opened the door. Outside were two uniformed French policemen, both nervously holding revolvers. In the background were Mesdames Marcourt and Salbert, clutching their dressing-gowns and whispering furiously. He thought he caught the word *espion*. Really! How absurd could the French get?

'So you've decided to come quietly', said one of the policemen, pocketing his revolver and advancing into the room. 'Excellent. Get dressed as quickly as possible.' He turned to his colleague. 'You pack his things.'

'What's all this about?' asked Henry. 'Why are you arresting me?'

'Just get dressed', said the first policemen. 'You'll find out soon enough.' He picked up the jacket of Henry's grey suit, and pulled out the wallet: it contained the 500,000 francs Henry had won racing, and the man whistled as he examined the thick roll of notes.

'One is well provided, I see.' He pocketed the wallet. 'Don't worry—you'll get a receipt for it.'

Henry began to dress. Ought he to ask for the man's warrant? In Britain, certainly: but this was France. A warrant was probably not required, and in any case, he had heard that the French police were quite capable of beating up anyone who tried to resist arrest. He decided to do as he was told.

Five minutes later, he was sandwiched between the two policemen in the back of a police-car racing across to the right bank. It stopped outside a large, grey stone building in the Rue St Honoré. Although it was six o'clock in the morning, all the lights were on. Henry got out and was hurried across the pavement. At the entrance a riot policeman, with fixed bayonet, waved them inside. The building was obviously a ministry, not a police-station: a uniformed commissionaire stood inside the door. They took a lift to the third floor, and then walked along a heavily carpeted corridor and into a large office, lavishly furnished with gilt chairs and desks. Several young men, who did not look at all like civil servants, lounged around.

'The minister is in?' asked the senior policeman. One of the young men nodded and jerked his thumb at a door at the far side of the room. 'Go straight in. He's waiting for you.'

Inside the inner office, sitting behind a massive nineteenth-century desk, and under a portrait of Louis Napoleon, was Count Nicol la Fouette, Minister of Economic Co-ordination. His plump, heavy-jowled, but still handsome face was tired but relaxed. He had taken off his coat and his tie, and his open-necked white shirt revealed a thick growth of black hair on his chest and a gold St. Christopher medal. In one hand was a ham sandwich, in the other an electric razor which he was running over the heavy growth on his cheeks. When Henry was brought in, he put down the sandwich and sat back in his chair.

'So you are the young man who's been making a fool of my daughter', he said, coldly. 'At any other time, I think I would have shot you.'

'What do you mean?' asked Henry. 'Why have I been brought here?'

'It's quite pointless to try and bluff me, monsieur. We know all about you. Cleo has confessed everything. She even told us your code number—AL 305.'

'I don't know what you're talking about.'

'Don't try and deny you're a British agent', shouted la Fouette angrily. 'Immediately we discovered the microphone and traced it to Cleo's room, she burst into tears, poor darling, and told me how you'd persuaded her to work for the British government. Since then, we've found out a lot of other things about you.' He waved a dossier of papers on his desk. 'You joined the staff of *France-Miracle*, in order to get access to the Quai d'Orsay. Information was received by the Quai d'Orsay as to the real nature of your activities. Unfortunately, no action was taken. Why? Because your superior, Sir Rupert Fitzhoward, is also, as we have suspected for some time, a British agent.'

'It's not true', said Henry. 'Sir Rupert merely got my name wrong. He's very absent-minded. He thinks I'm called Charles something, and when Taxim wrote to him about me, he thought Taxim had simply made a mistake.'

'You expect me to believe that?' stormed the Count. 'There is a great deal of other evidence against you. Only a trained operative could have set up the hidden microphone in my home. You planned to take recordings of my conversation which touched on secret government business, and send it to Whitehall. Several of the residents at your hotel, including the proprietress, who has been watching you for some time, have made depositions. They tally exactly with what my daughter told me.'

'Cleo's lying', said Henry bitterly. 'She persuaded me to help to record your conversations, so we could have the details of your *coup d'état* published in the Communist press. What she told you is rubbish. Why don't you bring her here and get her to tell the truth?'

'Don't mention her name! You used your odious charm to involve her in your schemes, and you have the insolence now to claim that she is lying. She has had a nervous breakdown and I've sent her down to the country to recuperate. You will never see her again, *monsieur*.'

'You can't hold me here', said Henry. 'I insist you telephone the British embassy. They'll tell you what nonsense all this is.'

'We have already spoken to them. Naturally, they deny all knowledge of you. Or, for that matter, of the tape-recording, which of course you have already delivered to them.'

'It's a lie. It's in Communist Party headquarters.'

'I am satisfied that you visited the embassy late last night. Somebody, whose description closely resembles yours, was seen to enter a side door of the Chancellry at about eleven-thirty.'

'You can't possibly prove this fantastic tale.'

'Unfortunately, we shall not have the opportunity. In the present state of Anglo-French relations, it is impossible for us to take any action beyond registering a strong confidential protest to your government and deporting you immediately.' He turned to the policeman. 'Did you search his things?'

'Yes, Monsieur le Ministre. He's covered his traces pretty well. We found nothing suspicious beyond a large sum of money—about 500,000 francs.'

'Return it to him. Are his bags packed?'

'Yes, Monsieur le Ministre.'

'Good.' He looked at his watch. 'The boat train for London leaves at nine. Take him to the Gare du Nord and hold him there until immediately before the train starts. I'll arrange for a plain-clothes escort to pick him up and escort him as far as the boat.' He turned to Henry again. 'You will never be permitted to return to France, monsieur. And you can tell your superiors that possession of the tape-recording is quite useless to them. We shall simply deny its authenticity if any attempt is made to use it.' His voice rose. 'And to-day, you can tell them, France will invest a strong government, led by a man of destiny, who will assert France's rights. There will be no more interference in our internal affairs. In future, Perfidious Albion will have to treat our country with respect! Now take him away.'

At the door, Henry paused, and turned round. Since the whole of this absurd incident had been built on a tissue of lies—springing originally from Michael Crick's anonymous letter—he though he might as well add another, and even the score. 'You're quite wrong about Sir Rupert being in league with me', he said. 'He knew nothing about my activities.'

'So you admit them!'

'Of course. Why not? My contact, if you really want to know, is a man called Crick. You'll find him at the Georges Cinq.'

At the Gard du Nord, Henry was handed over to two plain-clothes policemen, and all three had breakfast—hard-boiled eggs and coffee. In the train, they occupied a reserved first-class compartment, and played cards. The detectives were excessively courteous, even deferential. At Calais, they escorted him to the gangway of the ship, and handed him back his passport with a flourish.

'*Bon voyage*, monsieur', said the first. 'It has been a pleasure to make the acquaintance of one of your *métier*.'

'*Franchement*, I envy you your job', said the second. 'And so young, too, for such responsibility. Evidently, you are a man of talent.'

As the ship moved off, a commercial-looking gent joined Henry at the rail and nudged his elbow.

'I saw you were put aboard by two plain-clothes types', he said. ' 'ad a spot of trouble, 'ave you?'

'Yes', said Henry. 'I've been deported for spying.'

'Now then,' said the man. 'Don't give me that. You look more like a white slaver, you do. Come down below for a Guinness and tell me all about it.'

'All right', said Henry.

In the bar, the first people they saw were Edgar and Dora. Edgar's blue suit looked a bit crumpled, but Dora was as fresh and bosomy as ever in a white linen dress. They were drinking Whisky Sours.

'Hello', said Edgar. 'Going to London?'

'Yes', said Henry. 'I've been deported for spying.'

'How extraordinary. So have I. Not for spying, though. The police decided to crack down on my poor old publisher. Just because De Gaulle's coming back to power, you know. Right-wing régimes always start off in a puritanical mood. It never lasts, of course. So Skorsky's in gaol and I've been given the push. Spent last night in the cells, as you can see. Very annoying. Just when I'd got my hands on the profit side of the business.'

'Poor thing', said Dora solicitously, stroking his cheek. 'He's had a rough time, haven't you darling. So I decided I'd come along too.'

' 'ere', said the commercial gent. 'What *is* all this, a conspiracy?'

'Yes', said Henry. 'By the French. They've all suddenly gone mad. Let's have some drinks'. He waved to the barman.

'That's right what you said about the French', said the commercial gent thoughtfully, when their drinks arrived. 'Very unpredictable people, they are. Well, 'ere's mud in your eye.'

Several rounds of drinks later, the commercial gent was rubbing his knee against Dora, and Edgar had settled down to write a poem—'The Return of the Outcast'. Henry went on deck. The thin white line of the cliffs of Dover were just coming into view, and for the first time since he was at prep-school, Henry felt his chest swell with patriotic emotion. How wonderful to be back in England, land of sanity, moderation and common-sense! In retrospect, his entire life for the past few weeks had been a ludicrous and embarrassing nightmare. He had come to Paris to study French civilization: instead, he had been chased by policemen and Communists, involved in ferocious fights, prostituted himself working for a foreign propaganda magazine, been dragged, against his will, into an absurd conspiracy, denounced by secret informers, betrayed by the woman he loved and finally arrested and ignominiously expelled. He had learnt virtually nothing about French culture, but a great deal about the people who created it: their rudeness, their hysteria, their undependability, their dotty political parties, their Anglophobia, their obsession with spies, sex, plots and revolutions, above all their extraordinary gullibility. No wonder they had to change their system of government every few years!

What hurt, however, was not the way the French as a nation had behaved towards him—indefensible though this had been—but Cleo's betrayal. As soon as her father had discovered the microphone, she had not only panicked: she had promptly put all the blame on his shoulders and, for no conceivable reason other than sheer French bloody-mindedness, concocted a ridiculous story about his being a British agent. He had thought her a remarkable young woman, tough, purposeful, exceptionally intelligent; he had been in love with her, wanted desperately to marry her; jeopardized his career for her sake. But in the end she had turned out to be just a silly, romantic young girl, who had probably read too much Françoise Sagan. She had clearly never been in love with him: the whole episode had been a humiliating fiasco. The only good thing to be said for his stay in Paris was that it had finally made his mind up. No living in garrets for him. No descent into the dark tunnel in search of the gleam at the end. For a few days, under Cleo's spell, he had thought he would choose a life of excitement and passion. But now he knew: all he wanted was stability, security and peace. A brokerage at Lloyd's would suit him down to the ground.

The White Cliffs loomed nearer: Henry could make out tiny red-brick houses, a pub, a Morris Oxford, a group of workmen settling down to make tea. How reassuring it all seemed! Edgar joined him at the rail.

'I see you are feasting your eyes on the placid English scene. Does it rejoice your bourgeois soul?'

'It certainly does', said Henry vehemently. 'And don't make any more cracks about being a bourgeois. I'm proud to be one. Give me bourgeois England! The England of *Times* leaders and Rattigan plays, of licensing hours and nice, sensible debates on the Flick Knife Bill, the England of Stephen Potter and little Prince Charles, Arthur Bryant, the Old Vic, test matches, holidays at Bournemouth, the R.S.P.C.A. . . .'

'Selwyn Lloyd's England', said Edgar.

'Yes—him too. I love 'em all. Rainy Sundays, Lyons Corner Houses, trade union knights, crossword puzzles, Lady Docker, Godfrey Winn . . . ?'

'Steak and kidney pudding, J. B. Priestley, Billy Butlin, comprehensive schools, Jodrell Bank . . .'

'. . . debutantes.'

'. . . and dirty old men in Public Conveniences.'

'Colin Wilson, Enid Blyton, the Third Programme.'

'Sir Reginald Manningham-Buller—you mustn't forget him.'

'Certainly not. Nor Mr. William Johnston Keswick.'

'Handel's *Messiah*, conducted by Sir Malcolm Sargent.'

'Dr. Bronowski explaining the ineffable.'

'Sir William Haley writing on Trollope.'

'Sefton Delmer surveying the international scene.'

'The Y.M.C.A.'

'The National Coal Board.'

'. . . and thousands and thousands of schoolgirls, all trying to look like Lolita. . . .'

The ship bumped heavily against the quay.

'Normalcy', said Henry softly. 'Normalcy.'

'This is Dover', said the ship's Tannoy, 'have your landing-cards and passports ready, please.'

They trudged off the boat, Edgar weighed down beneath Dora's luggage. There were no porters. In the customs shed, a customs officer unearthed Henry's books with relish.

'What's this? Proust, eh?' He peered laboriously at the pages, turning them over slowly after moistening his index finger.

'A very celebrated French author', said Henry. 'Available in all public libraries.'

'I've heard that before', said the customs officer. 'I'll have to check if it's on the list.'

He returned a few moments later, without the book.

'It's not on the list', he said, adding darkly, 'so we'll have to get it *read*.'

'Read away', said Henry, fastening his case. 'I never liked the bloody thing, anyway.'

'Now then, Sir, there's no cause to be abusive. I'm only doing my duty, and if people *will* buy French books. . . .'

'Exactly', said Henry. 'Why should they? A very good day to you, officer.'

'And to you too, Sir, I'm sure', said the man, mollified.

Henry joined Dora and Edgar in the vague no-man's-land between the customs and the station. In the distance, the train steamed softly, waiting.

'We'll have to carry our own bags', said Edgar. 'I haven't done so much manual labour since I was in the footer team at school.'

'I don't think we will', said Henry. 'Look.'

Bearing down towards them, black, massive, magisterial, was a Rolls-Royce. Madame Plympton's Rolls-Royce, in fact. And behind the wheel was Cleo.

It took Henry exactly five seconds to race to the car, wrench open the door, and take Cleo into his arms. She was trembling, and there were tears in her eyes.

'Darling', she said. 'Thank God I've found you. I wasn't certain whether you'd be on this boat. Are you all right? They didn't beat you?'

'No, no. But I don't understand any more. Why are you here? What happened?'

'The Communists double-crossed us. After you left the Carrefour de Châteaudun, they must have telephoned Papa and told him about the mike. They told him all about you, too.'

'The swine—he said that *you'd* told him. But why did

you cook up this nonsense about my being a British agent?'

'Don't you see? It was the only way I could save you from gaol. I knew that if I could convince them that you were working for the British, they wouldn't dare do anything more than extradite you. If I'd told them the truth, you could have been charged with *attente contre la sécurité du territoire* and sent to prison under the Emergency Regulations. They wouldn't believe me at first. Then Papa did a lot of telephoning, and came back with all sorts of evidence against you. I was astonished, and then I almost began to believe you *were* a secret agent, and that you'd been deceiving me all along. So I cried. You aren't, darling, are you?'

'Of course not. A dreadful man I'd annoyed sent an anonymous letter to the Quai d'Orsay, that's all. I suppose it's rather lucky he did, looking back on it. Darling, I owe you an apology. I've been cursing you for a mean, treacherous bitch. Will you forgive me?'

She kissed him. 'That's your answer. I think I'd really forgive you anything. I thought, as I was coming across the Channel, that even if you were a British Agent, and had just been stringing me along all the time, that I still loved you. I decided I'd track you down in England and *make* you marry me.'

'But I still don't understand how you got here?'

'Darling, it was the trickiest thing I've ever done. Papa had me bundled into this car, and told the chauffeur to drive me down to our château in Normandy, and that I was to be kept there absolutely under lock and key. I pretended to be just a tired, frightened little girl, so he didn't send the detective with me. As soon as we got outside Paris and into the open country, I hit the chauffeur hard on the head with the heel of my shoe. He went out quite cold, poor thing. I tied him up with my stockings and dumped him by the side of the road.' She paused, pensively. 'I hope somebody's found him by now—he's such an obliging man, normally. Then I drove furiously for Dieppe. I was going to catch the boat, but I suddenly remembered the air-ferry. Honor's not going to miss this car, I told myself, and the tryptique is in order, so why not fly it across? So I did, in a huge, fat aeroplane. The pilot was awfully nice, and allowed me to sit in the co-pilot's seat. I think I could easily learn to fly. He gave me lunch at the airport, and then he found out all about the arrival of boats and things. So I drove here, and I found you, and everything's right now, isn't it, and you're going to make an honest woman of me?'

'Yes', said Henry, 'Special Licence, Caxton Hall and all that. My God—what am I letting myself in for? You're the most terrifying, dangerous woman I've ever met.' He kissed her, running his fingers through the thick strands of her black hair, feeling the warm pressure of her body.

'You can't park 'ere', said a porter, who had suddenly appeared from nowhere. Neither Henry nor Cleo took any notice. 'Oh well, seeing as it's a Rolls', he added and shuffled off.

'Seeing as it's a Rolls', said Edgar's voice, 'and seeing that this touching little scene has gone on quite long enough, what about giving us two a lift to London?'

'I'm sorry', said Henry, releasing Cleo. 'I haven't introduced you. Cleo, this is Lady Treffle and Edgar the Poet. Fellow exiles from France. Can we take them to London?'

'Why not?' said Cleo. 'Provided they don't mind me driving at 160 kilometres an hour.'

They all climbed aboard, and Cleo drove out of the station yard on to the great, ancient road through Kent. There was silence for a few miles, then she turned to Henry.

'Don't you have something in England called the Labour Party?' she asked.

'Indeed yes—a most respectable body of opinion, somewhat Left of Centre. Like myself', he added.

'Exactly. It's about time I looked into it, don't you think?'

'Then God help Mr. Gaitskell', said Henry.

The car raced smoothly towards London, travelling at ninety miles an hour. The only noise was the ticking of the clock.